In Course of True Love

By the same author

It's No Longer a Dream

In Course of True Love

SANJEEV RANJAN

Srishti
PUBLISHERS & DISTRIBUTORS

Srishti Publishers & Distributors
Registered Office: N-16, C.R. Park
New Delhi – 110 019

Corporate Office: 212A, Peacock Lane
Shahpur Jat, New Delhi – 110 049
editorial@srishtipublishers.com

First published by
Srishti Publishers & Distributors in 2012

Revised impression, 2017

10 9 8 7 6 5 4 3 2 1

This is a work of fiction. The characters, places, organisations and events described in this book are either a work of the author's imagination or have been used fictitiously. Any resemblance to people, living or dead, places, events, communities or organisations is purely coincidental.

The author asserts the moral right to be identified as the author of this work.

Printed and bound in India

To my parents for their love and support,

*Ashima Kapoor, and Ritika Dey**

**For giving some unforgettable moments to Aarush's life.*

"She walks in beauty, like the night
Of cloudless climes and starry skies,
And all that's best of dark and bright
Meet in her aspect and her eyes..."

— Lord Byron

"Mai jahan rahoon, mai kahin bhi hoon,
teri yaad saath hai,
Kisi se kahoon, ke nahi kahoon,
ye jo dil ki baat hai..."

—A song from Namaste London

"Love is the best thing when you have it. But when things go wrong, it hurts... torments the mind and makes you cry copiously. Nothing can be worse than this. It is painful."

Author's note and Acknowledgments

It gives me immense pleasure in presenting this novel to you. This novel is very close to me and my life. Writing this novel was both a joy and a challenge for me. Most of the incidents in this novel are based on my life events. But this journey to complete the novel, to capture all my emotions and feelings was, indeed, not so easy. While writing, I was accompanied by several great souls who helped me through this journey.

To start with, I would like to thank Nachiket Pal, a very good friend, who constantly supported me in my rough days, acted as a pillar of support, read my scripts, and gave various invaluable suggestions.

Also my sincere thanks to Ahmed Faiyaz, Pratik D. Upadhayay, Ankit Uttam, Chandan Kumar, Priyanshu Raj and Rakesh Kumar for their valuable suggestions.

I will be forever grateful to Mrs Pramila Natrajan ma'am, professor of Sastra University, and Mr Thankachand sir, my English Teacher who, in spite of their busy schedules, spent their time in suggesting and editing a few chapters.

I would like to thank the editors at Wiser Literary for their effort in editing the script.

I would like to show my gratefulness to some of the world famous authors and coaches – Robin Sharma, Shiv Khera, and

Rhonda Byrne – who unknowingly mentored me through their words which always imbued my veins with positive energy and pushed me to chase my dream.

On the publishing front, I would like to thank Mr Jayanta Kumar Bose, who gave me a chance to present my thoughts in the form of this novel and the whole team at Srishti for helping me at every stage.

Last of all, my deepest and most sincere thanks to all those who remained connected to me and encouraged me knowingly or unknowingly while I was writing this book, and to all my readers.

1

28th April, 2008
3:00 p.m.

It has been ten months since that brooding June of last summer. I still remember everything before it vanished into my other memories. I still remember that moment of pain when my relationship shattered in front of my own eyes, and my love walked away from me.

I've arrived at a stage in my life where I'm actually going through the burden of certain memories. The way it intensifies as time goes by, it leaves me shattered. The worst feeling is to see the memories of your happiest moments giving you the most terrible nightmares you've ever had. People say if you treat your past with nonchalance, it won't taint your present. I don't know how true this is, but my past – which I have tried to bury to keep the tendrils of those thoughts out of my mind and out of my heart with great effort – still claws its way out.

Looking back at my life now, I realize how I still peek into that deserted and baseless relationship; that seed of hope which I have planted in the desert of ruin, which I nurtured with my love, with my honest feelings, but it could only reap fruits of nostalgic pain for me. The pain of love is still flowing in my veins, the pain that I am carrying today and going back home with.

"Where are Manav and Saksham? They are so irresponsible.

"They haven't even put their bags on the top of the bus?" Firoz says, frowning at me. "The bus is about to leave in five minutes."

"I don't know. I haven't seen them for the last ten minutes. Maybe, they are around some cold drinks shop," I say quietly. I look around but can't see them anywhere.

April in Bokaro is a very hot and torrid month. The sun is fierce and almost parches the earth. Sometimes it hides in the clouds and peeps out after a moment. Rains are intermittent and even when they do fall, it is only to break this heat. A short spell of rain every two days, sometimes three, providing some momentary relief from the incessant heat. But today, there seems to be no sign of rain. It is around 3:00 p.m. and the sun is still high, beating down mercilessly on our heads.

"I will go and look for Saksham and Manav," I say to Firoz, moving forward to start the pursuit.

After crossing the labyrinth of the road, I catch sight of them and I know I was correct about them. They are indeed at one of the small cold drinks shops with a gabled roof. I take long strides to reach them quickly.

"The conductor is asking if you two have tied your luggage either on the top of the bus or at the back," I say, panting and breathless, placing my hand on Saksham's shoulder. The two of them stop talking and look at me. They grunt. Their grave look makes my hand slip. "If you have any more bags to load, hurry and load them up. The bus is about to move out. Come soon."

They do not say a word and continue sipping their drinks. I buy water bottles and leave the place. It always vexes me when I don't get a reply, not even a nod, leave aside a word.

Things are not the same as they used to be. Everyone and everything has changed. The two of them, Manav and Saksham, were once my best friends but today, they don't even speak to me properly. I don't know the reasons except that there is a rift in our friendship. The closeness we once shared is no more. Two years, and everything has changed so drastically. Despite every change, one thing has never changed, and will remain forever – my love for her, my feelings for her. One thing never drifted away – my mind away from her. The images are forever etched in my mind.

By the time I return, people have already started boarding the bus. I rush towards the bus. Firoz is already on his seat. I settle down a little far from them, a few rows behind. They booked my ticket without letting me know. Soon, they were engaged in a conversation. I look over at them, but no one cares to look back at me.

As the bus accelerates my heart starts beating faster and a pang of nostalgia envelops me. I tilt my head towards the windowpane through which the sun rays are still streaming. They fall over me soothingly, though with less intensity.

Two days ago, AIEEE, a nation-wide examination, was conducted and we'd then decided to leave Bokaro.

The bus resumes its jerky motion. Thick clusters of trees, plants, shrubs, weeds, shacks, and some pakka houses start passing by, trailing along the roads which brought me here two years ago. I keep my head inclined to the pane, looking out with sullen eyes. After a few moments, I take out my mobile phone but can find neither a message nor a single missed call. Two years in Bokaro has impoverished my life. Can anyone at least convey to her that I am leaving Bokaro? Does she know this? I know it is of no use to ask these questions to myself. After staring at the screen for another moment, I open the saved messages folder to read the same message, which she had sent me in the month of October. I don't know how many times I have read this message till now.

COURT ORDER! You are accused of crawling into my heart and hijacking my smile with your cute behavior. You are sentenced to be my love for life time. NO BAIL.

My droopy lower lip stretches upward into a weak smile. Hope is being destroyed with every inch the bus moves away, with every jerk. I am pained with the intensity of the yearning for her, and the pain of not meeting her at least once, for the last time, as today is my last day in Bokaro. While I was here, there was hope that I could see her once, may be in a market. But even that couldn't survive my hard luck. Distance is a dangerous thing. It changes everything.

I close my eyes slowly, my head still tilted towards the pane. Soon, my mind swarms with something joyous. It flashes something sweet and lovely.

Lashed hazel eyes, the pink cheeks and lips, the colour of ripe pomegranate, smiling cutely in the class.

I open my eyes after sometime as it becomes too unbearable to remember those things. It is true that I can't forget her. I look out, everything is left behind. I am going away from her, from Bokaro. May be forever, carrying a pain, shattered dreams, and those memories. Whatever happened, I don't know. My only wish is to live with her, with our dreams. There is still a soft corner for her in my heart. I look back; the bus is leaving everything behind rapidly. I wish I could do the same. I remember the time two years back, when the same bus was heading in the reverse direction, entering the city, making a destination for me, to find my awaiting love; both of us being two different personalities. Tears flow down my cheeks. Everything seems like it had happened yesterday.

Life is too short. Everything which we build in years, shatters in seconds and leaves behind a debris of memories, dreams and emotions. Those moments which I have captured, still flow in my body. I can still feel them, though she is not with me now. Though so much time has passed without her, her presence never faded completely. It recedes partially because it is painful to remember those things, those days, which bring tears with a whisper, "Please come back! Please make everything beautiful as before."

I pick out my diary, turn open the first page. A big, red heart with an arrow pierced through it stares back at me. I drew it nearly two years ago. At the top of the page, it is written – an intriguing love journey of a shy, introvert Aarush and bold, smart, beautiful and open-minded Ashima Kapoor. Tears stream down endlessly.

I turn over to the next page.

It starts on a morning, two years back.

Everything I remember still brings a new life to me. That morning which marked the beginning of my life and I fade into the past.

2

25th May 2006

I woke up with a jerk. "What time is it?" I skewed my eye over the clock; it was 4:45 a.m. I simply sat there on my bed, staring outside. The surroundings were still in the lap of darkness. I lay there, drenched in sweat, looking up at the ceiling. No power, I realized. The electric fan hanged still. And there was nothing one could do at that odd hour except sleep; so I did.

Trin, trin...

I thumped my hand hard to switch off the alarm clock that was perforating my eardrums. I couldn't control my anger as I was having a really lovely dream. I just sat on my bed, sulking over having set the alarm for so early. I yawned aloud and got off my bed, looking around.

I belong to a middle class family and accordingly, my room was poorly furnished. Though my condition was fairly noble with the room and the covers all well cleaned. The furniture consisted of two chairs and a table in a corner beside the door. In the other three corners of the room, there was a trunk on which a TV set was placed, a door connecting my room with the other parts of the house and my bed.

All the light and air in the room came in from the window lone window, covered with a thin curtain. The wall had a dull look;

most of it was covered with either numerous posters or calendars. I often argue that every calendar showed the same date. But no one ever listened to me. Instead, I would be told things such as- 'This particular calendar was given by some bank while the other one was given by a pundit ji ... And that one was given by ...' Indeed, every Diwali, a newer poster would be stuck to the wall. It was done to increase the beauty of the wall, according to my other family members, especially my mother.

At times, she behaved in a very strange and unusual manner. She would beat me up mercilessly even for my little mistakes. I always had a feeling that she never really loved me like other children's mothers. Even at a younger age, most of the time, I used to wash my own clothes and serve myself my meals from the kitchen. Almost once in every three days, we used to get into severe arguments and wouldn't talk to each other for weeks. After one such argument, we hadn't talked for months together. She never truly supported me in any of my accomplishments; hadn't praised me even when I had scored more than ninety percent in my examinations. And it was on that day that I wondered if she was indeed not my mother. I could after all, have been her step son. I would never know the truth.

I had never actually known the meaning of love. To pamper myself with love and emotional longings, I used to watch movies or read magazines. It was only in movies that I would see how someone cared for you and you too adored her back, someone would wish on your birthday and make the day special for you. But, all that was only a dream for me. I could easily remember that my birthday was celebrated like any other normal day. No wishes. No new clothes. No cake. No gifts. No smiles. No happiness. I thought I'd never know if anyone would ever care for me. At times, I used to brood over all this, alone on the roof, and used to find myself lonely.

My tenth board examinations were finished.

I stumbled out into the balcony, still yawning profoundly, as I had no habit of waking up so early. I looked around drowsily; there was a wide emptiness over the road. I just crawled towards the corridor on the third floor. Due to walking up so early, I had a hint of frustration on my face. But, after a few minutes, my feelings of frustration and unsettlement were replaced with an undefined satisfaction as I stared at the road, the emptiness and silence of which matched with my life. I realized that there was something like me out there too. The wind was blowing gently and was rushing towards me from every direction. The sweat on my body soon disappeared in the cool breeze. Soon, I started feeling good and spent a few more minutes enjoying the breeze.

My father had gone out of station the previous night itself.

I walked back into my room and inserted a DVD of Harry Potter, switching on the television.

I was watching with deep concentration when suddenly someone's angry yell broke the silence. It was my mom. That meant only one thing to me; the whole day was going to be the same – screaming and screaming all day long.

"What?" I said furiously, without moving my eyes off the television screen.

She yelled back that Saksham had been calling out for me for the last five minutes. Quietly, I rushed out of the room.

The sun was on its way to start a new day as usual, but clouds were hovering in the sky.

"Aarush, where are you man? I have been shouting for the last fifteen minutes!" He sounded annoyed. "All your neighbours have come out, but you didn't." He looked a little flustered.

"Ok … It's early in the morning. What's the matter?" I asked.

"Could you please come down?" he said, now in a softer tone, though his eyes still had that glint of fury.

He was in a white T-shirt and blue bermudas. His dishevelled hair, pale eyes indicated that he had come straight from his bedroom.

"The results have been declared," he mumbled.

"Oh, yes! I almost forgot!" I murmured. "How could I forget?" I thought, exasperated at myself. My heart started pounding; my mind started hovering, anxious to know the results. My eyes were fixed upon his lips, waiting to hear the results, hands clenched into fists now.

"You got 90.8%," he said with a plain look. Listening to this, I was plainly baffled, because I had expected a lot more than that. Instead, I began to ponder about how I could have gotten such low marks. I had done my real best in all the examinations. I didn't have an answer for this doubt.

"What about you?" I enquired.

"I got 89.8%," he said in a sad tone. I knew he too wasn't happy with his result.

"What about the others?" I asked again.

He said, "Not so great. Firoz got 89%, Manav scored 88.8%." I was really surprised now, as they too were expecting better marks, just like me.

"Come on, let's go to school and collect our certificates," he continued.

"Yes, of course," I said. "Meet you in half an hour." He left, agreeing.

Saksham was one of my oldest friends. I couldn't remember when our friendship had begun. Maybe, in class seventh when I had joined DAV School. We played together. He stayed at a walkable distance from my home. He was with me in my school too and we were good friends.

On entering the room, my mother asked, "What is the matter? Why has Saksham come? It's so early."

"The results have been declared. I got 90.8%," I mumbled slowly.

She said, "Less than we expected." Her face was no longer illuminated. She tried to conceal her anger. I always sensed it when she tried to hide her disgust.

Even 98% is not very good for you, I thought.

My father called to know the result. I explained everything to him and he said he would come in the evening and discuss it. After having breakfast, I went to the school with Saksham. Firoz and Manav met us later. Every one of us was unhappy.

"So, you are taking admission in Computer Science?" Firoz asked.

I replied, "Yes".

Well, as Siwan was not a good place for higher education, I had decided to go to Bokaro, following the advice given by Priyesh.

We entered the school and collected every document. It took us around four hours. I came back home at 2:30 p.m. We had decided to leave Siwan in two days. I told my mother everything about our plan as my parents had already decided to send me to another place for my higher studies. My father reached home later that night.

"Your marks are fine, but you have scored less in Sanskrit and English," Papa said.

I nodded in agreement.

My mother was standing beside me. She had expected more than 95%. A long discussion was held and finally, it was decided that I would be going to Bokaro. Actually, money was a bit of a problem for my family. So, my father was slightly worried about sending me so far away. Nevertheless, he was determined to send me to Bokaro. I knew he would be ready for any sacrifice. And this made me feel responsible. My father has always loved me. My mother also approved of the idea by simply nodding with a barren face. I called my friends to book the tickets. My father talked to Priyesh about Bokaro and the admissions there. He was a good friend of mine. He lived just two blocks away from my house. He was senior to me and was already in Bokaro.

I packed my suitcase and a small bag. I packed the basic essentials like towel, soaps, clothes, a brush, and, most importantly, the certificates and was ready to step into a new phase.

3

On the scheduled date, we left Siwan for Bokaro, to start a new life. We boarded a bus at 2:00 p.m. Everyone's parents had come to see off their children. The time of last minute instructions had finally arrived as we were leaving the city for the first time. To my surprise, my mother too accompanied us to the bus stand.

My father came over to me. "Listen son, I have worked hard to keep you happy and to satisfy your every need. We have a lot of expectations from you and I know you will never disappoint us. Be careful with the money. You are going out of this town alone for the first time. You are at a very crucial juncture of life, as you have to handle everything by yourself from now onwards. So, you have to be really careful. You will be making new friends. Be very polite to them."

His words were cemented in my heart and soul.

"Hire a coolie after getting down there. I know your bags are too heavy. Don't try to carry everything by yourself. First, bargain and fix the price before letting him touch the luggage. Twenty rupees is more than enough. Have you kept the money in a safe place?" My father asked, standing outside and speaking to me through the window of the seat where I was sitting.

I nodded, trying hard not to become emotional. A single tear was on the verge of rolling down, but I got a grip over myself to avoid my parents from breaking into tears too, which I never wanted in the first place.

I got down from the bus and touched their feet for their blessings. With nothing much to say, I boarded back and settled near the window seat again with a feeling of a void.

Soon, the conductor blew his whistle, indicating the driver to start the bus. It started with a sudden jerk, its horn honking in a screeching tone. And the bus crept forward. My parents started taking long strides to keep pace with the vehicle. They kept advising me about various things, though soon they were left behind as the bus accelerated. We waved to our parents. After a few seconds, they were swept away, out of my sight.

We all had booked our seats together. I noticed that everyone was silent. I have never really liked staying quiet for too long.

Later, Firoz was the first one to come out of this stupor. He started cracking a few cheap jokes, though Manav and Saksham chose to stay quiet.

Soon, dusk fell, followed by night. I took out my tiffin box and we had an eating session, after which, I resumed staring dreamily out through the window imagining about Bokaro – its environment and everything else.

It was a long journey, spanning almost an entire night as our bus, which was not fully loaded sped along.

The next morning, at nearly 4:00 a.m, we reached Naya Mode, the bus stand. The bus screeched to a halt and all the passengers jerked forward and hit the seats before them. "Foolish driver. Can't he stop slowly?" someone cried out from behind.

Even I was annoyed and started rubbing my forehead, staring out at the surroundings. It was as dark as night. Only a few people could be seen out for walks, including the bus conductor who was relentlessly shouting like an animal, hitting the bus from time to time, "Wake up and come out. Bokaro! We have reached Bokaro! Bokaro!."

I woke up Firoz, Manav and Saksham. "Wake up. We have reached Bokaro."

"It's too early! How can we reach so fast? Aftab bhaiya said the bus would reach at around 5 a.m. Just have a look outside, It's still night," Firoz moaned and cuddled up in his seat, pulling the sheet tighter over him.

"It is four in the morning and we have reached an hour earlier than the usual time. Wake up!" I said. Finally, they were completely out of their drowsiness and pulled down their baggage from the upper shelf.

I got down from the bus, ready to write my own destiny. There was something in the fresh air, giving me a new pleasure and urging me to enter and start a new life among new students and strange people.

Only a few buses had come into view till now. Our bus stood near the pavement that was full with night sleepers and autowallahs. Some coolies rushed forward while most of the others stood at their spots, believing their instincts that none of us was going to let them lift the bags. A slow breeze was blowing, giving us a sweet pleasure. I stretched out my muscles and yawned aloud. Eventually, all the others got down, carrying their bags.

The bus stand was surrounded with thick trees shrubs. At a distance, a street lamp was glowing, giving out a dim yellow light.

We hired an auto for Jai Jawan Petrol Pump.

We reached the exact spot where Aftab bhaiya was waiting to receive us. He had a good physique with robust shoulders. His face was small and round with small eyes.

I just looked around. Needless to say, the road was clean and wide, shadowed with trees on both sides, and was properly maintained, unlike in Siwan. A few people were jogging, while birds were chirping. The houses had been built in a row, unlike the ones in Siwan, all the buildings possessing same constructional design and colour.

Aftab, Priyesh, Animesh and Ritesh were good friends and a year senior to us. All our seniors had qualified from the same school as ours. They knew Manav and Firoz. Also, Manav and Ritesh were brothers. So, they knew me through my friends. Aftab and Firoz were in Chinmaya, and Ritesh and Animesh were in Aayappa. We reached the flat within a couple of minutes. It was on the second floor. I looked around it. It had two adjacent rooms. To the side of one room there was a kitchen, while beside the other was a bathroom and a big room with three beds where we were going to stay. To me, the room looked charming and better than my expectations. It was even better than my own home. Saksham was to stay in the other room. His roommate was a boy named Mayank from Dhanbad.

I freshened up and arranged my luggage in a hustle, placing the mattress on the bed and picking out the shorts, towel and other necessary items.

"You all look sleepy. Get some rest. I know travelling in the bus along such a road is too hectic. Just tell me what you would like for lunch. I will do one thing then, I shall order themess wallah to bring four more tiffin boxes," Aftab bhaiya said.

"How is the food here?" Firoz asked.

"Not as tasty as it is at your homes. They sometimes put anything and everything in it. I have warned and abused them so many times. I have even shifted the services, but they all are the same. Their caterers are all trained to put in little money while the rest is put into their bellies. The only thing you get to do is you either choose vegetarian or non-vegetarian," he said, looking at me.

"I am not very fussy about food, but I'd like to choose non-vegetarian," I said. The other three chose non-vegetarian too.

He laughed. I started wondering what could be so funny until he explained, "Actually, both are almost similar except that there's a slightly different taste." And he left, leaving us to have a quick nap.

When we woke up, the mess wallah had already delivered the food. I washed my face and went over to Ritesh bhaiya's room.

I opened the tiffin box. It had rice, dal and some green messy vegetable. I ate it as I was famished without any complaints owing to the strain on my face. I kept the box aside after I was done, had a little chat and returned to my room.

◆

"You know they are planning things for ragging and discussing something of that sort?" Firoz came over after some time and informed me and Manav. "At night."

"Oh, no," I said. My heart sank at the word 'ragging'. I had often seen on television how some students had committed suicide after getting tormented and tortured by their seniors. My heart pained and I was scared.

"This is not a college. Haven't they grown up yet? They are educated people. And, don't they even realize that this leads to physical and mental frustrations? What would they ask us to do, anyway? An act of begging or an introduction or dance? Nothing more than that, right?"

"Yeah ... maybe." Firoz was smiling as if he has been offered a treat.

Later, everybody slipped into another round of sleep while I unpacked my bag.

Dusk was falling. Though the others were still sleeping and it was already too late. I felt too excited to sleep. I walked out, making my way through a narrow street, passing by a cinema hall and sauntering towards the next road. This road led me to the main market, city centre, which I realized when I saw a series of small shops. The roads and the market were shadowed by vivid arc lamps that were glowing with dim yellow lights. I then made my way through the small stall of golgappe, towards a big circular cavernous space with the numerous parked vehicles. There were shops all around the place while, in one corner, there were several egg roll stalls, the vendors of which were persistently shouting and calling out for their customers. People were arriving in their cars, parking them hurriedly to start off their shopping session. I was thrilled at seeing this crowd and babble. Unlike Siwan, cars, scooters, motorbikes and auto-rickshaws were not jostling for space on the road. Needless to say, the road was not pounded with too many people as it used to be in Siwan. It was quiet and calm – the two things which I had been searching in my life till date. Sometimes, the honking of a car broke the tranquility of the ambience and its serenity. I was too tired to go to the hostel immediately. So, I settled down at a corner for some time before starting my stroll again, staring at the big hoardings.

As predicted, that night after dinner, seniors foisted on us to do things. I stood right behind Firoz, trying to hide myself. All our seniors were sitting abreast on the chairs in the hall.

"First of all, each one of you come forward and introduce yourself in Hindi, not a single word of English is accepted. Every time you speak an English word, a cloth would be stripped off your bodies," Aftab bhaiya bellowed. It seemed like an army leader was warning and giving instructions to his team before the beginning of a battle.

Firoz stepped forward to lead the campaign and started introducing himself. He used two English words, making him lose his shirt and vest. I reassured myself and carefully gave out my introduction, but did one foolish mistake at the end. After the introduction was given, I uttered 'thanks'. It slipped out casually, as I was already happy that I wouldn't have to shed my shame in front of these shameless seniors. I was asked to take off my shirt alone. Saksham made too many mistakes and finally ended up in his underpants. Manav carefully completed his task, without having to strip anything.

"Ah, good performance," Aftab bhaiya said. "Let's give them a big round of applause." All his cronies brayed with laughter. Upon hearing the next task, my eyes dilated with severe shame. "All of you have to walk in a line, like models do in their fashion shows." At first, Firoz smiled at hearing this, but the next moment his smile vanished when he heard the senior's next words, "Only in your underwear."

We stood frozen and started whispering amongst us. I protested.

"What happened? What are you all discussing?" Ritesh bhaiya called out this time.

"Ah, I think they are feeling shy," Aditya bhaiya interrupted. "Come on!"

Seniors made us do it, anyway. They dragged me from the room into the hall. At that moment, I took up a firm decision never to mingle with this group and to keep myself away from all the seniors, except Priyesh. Finally, I stripped my clothes and appeared in my underwear, like all other boys. We did the ramp walk, feeling more ashamed than ever. My eyes were downcast, brimming with anger. After that session, I refused to do the other tasks and went to sleep. All the others followed my lead.

◆

"Get up and get ready! We will have to go to the school for your admissions. These are forms to be filled up by you all," Aftab bhaiya said, placing the forms on my bed the next morning. "Take care you make no mistake while filling them."

We filled our forms carefully. One could easily sense our excitement.

We went to Chinmaya Vidyalaya. It was quite a big school. A vast, green ground was on the left side, while a snake-like row of yellow buses stood on the other. On them imprinted in blue was the name 'Chinmaya'. There was a wide open area in front of the building. A long queue stood near the counter. We went over and joined the queue.

After a few minutes, I heard someone calling out.

"Those who have scored more than 90% as an aggregate, please come out of line. They can attend the direct interview round." Someone, short and bald approached the queue and announced.

"And what about the others?" Firoz asked. One could easily discern his tension.

"They will have to wait in line. They will be called later as per the percentage."

I stepped out of the queue, looked around and noticed that about twenty others did so too. We were directed into the office by the same person.

After twenty long minutes of impatient and tensed waiting, they finally called out my name.

I entered the room and looked around; there were three teachers seated behind a table.

They indicated to me to sit on a chair. I did, passing the filled form, and maintaining a calm and placid face while they checked my form.

"Science 98, Math 96 ... That's good," one of them said. "Impressive."

I smiled. They asked me a few questions. I answered them patiently and correctly. By their relaxed expressions, it seemed that they were satisfied with my answers. They had a few seconds of whispered conversation before passing the form and saying, "We give you section C." The same section that I had applied for – Computer Science.

"Thanks sir. Thank you very much," I responded with joy and hurriedly came out.

I called papa to tell him about my admission. My parents sighed in relief upon hearing the news that I got admitted in a top school.

I looked around but couldn't find anyone familiar. There was that long queue still. Parents were instructing their wards regarding how to talk to teachers and how to answer. I smiled. I had passed that phase and had been successful in getting an admission in the second best school of Bokaro. Upon finding no one else, I came back to the hostel where, to my surprise, all the others were already in the room.

They told me that the cut-off for the admissions had been increased. Now, there seemed to be hardly a chance for Manav, who was silent all the while and looked deeply disappointed. I chose not to talk to him at the moment.

The next day, Firoz and Saksham got their admissions in the Sanskrit section. Unfortunately, Manav couldn't make it and he took admission in another school.

We also paid for our maths tuition. Our classes would start in twenty days. The tuitions too, at almost the same time. So, we came back to Siwan for a fortnight or so.

4

19th July 2006
3:55 p.m.

I was late. So, I rushed for my maths tuition. Usually, I would reach there just before the class would begin. My friends had already gotten there. When I finally reached the place, a flock of students were leaving the class, as the session for the previous batch had just finished. After a minute's scrutiny, I saw that none of my friends were there in that crowd. Realizing that they had gone upstairs, I rushed towards the class on the first floor, running along the staircase, throwing caution to the winds. I came to an abrupt halt in front of the class door. More than a hundred students were bustling near the doorway, as the students of previous batch tried to scurry out and the students of the upcoming batch tried to enter in their hurry to occupy the best seats. Girls were waiting for the crowd to clear so that they could enter the room leisurely. They were all sitting in the teacher's cabin, talking and giggling. I searched around for my friends in the corridor and, upon not finding them, I entered the room.

A few second later, I spotted my friends sitting on the second bench. I wandered over to them and took a seat beside Firoz.

Now and then, a few girls started entering the room and took their seats eventually.

A few minutes later, sir entered the room, wearing a red coloured shirt with a fleck of black patch, looking bizarre. Everyone was engaged in talking and nobody paid any attention to him.

He started teaching after cracking a few cheap jokes; that was how that class began every day. All were attentive except a few.

After around fifteen minutes, sir momentarily left the class to attend a phone call and stepped out into the balcony. He got such calls in almost every class. Maybe, it was his girlfriend as he was still single, I presumed.

I was just squinting around the class as the previous questions had already been solved and a new one was on the board.

When I was just about to turn towards the board again, my eyes suddenly got glued to a pair of beautiful eyes, lashed hazel eyes, which were staring at me.

She was Ashima. But how did I know her name?

◆

On the very first day of the tuition class, when I had reached the class early, the same mad dash for seats was going on. A boy, oval-faced, dark-complexioned with sticky hair, sitting on the bench near the door was reciting the girls' details to Firoz, who was sitting beside him. He was listening closely as they passed them one by one, and it was then that I heard her name.

"This is Sneha Gupta,

Chinmaya Vidyalaya,

Lives in sector 8. No boyfriend yet."

"Next, one is Ishika Ray.

Delhi Public School.

Live in sector 4 F. Two boyfriends already."

After a pause, he said, "And here comes the most pathakha or maal or whatever you all want to say … Ashima, the most beautiful and sexy." And he started ogling at her while the boys behind me started mocking, "Maal, item ..."

"Which school?" Firoz asked curiously.

"DPS. Lives in sector 4F. No one is sure if she has any boyfriend, but lots of others have been chasing her for years."

I raised my eyes to look at her. I couldn't see her properly as she had already taken her seat by then. I noticed that she was short, and I could see only a side of her face. I didn't try again for a better look as I had nothing to do with her then. That was the first time I ever saw her. Even then I never knew that this was the same girl whom I would love the most, perhaps more than my life.

"Next ... That pink one is Pavitra Verma and, right beside her, the blue one is Divya. Both are Ashima's close chaps. Also from DPS." I could distinctly recall that listening to these facts, while Firoz had felt sad that he wasn't a student of DPS.

◆

As she continued to stare at me, my face started turning red, aghast, and sweat broke on my forehead. I had a sensation of something unusual rising up. My heart started pounding harder. No one had ever stared at me that way before. I averted my gaze; the only thing that I could do at that moment.

I turned my face towards the board, trying to ignore her stare. "Is she still looking at me or it is merely a coincidence?" I asked myself out of curiosity. I tilted my face again to check for myself and stole a covert glance at her. "Oh my god, she is still looking at me." I again turned back, tried to concentrate on the problem on the board. When the class finally ended, I went back to my hostel quickly. A whisper of nameless surprise. I didn't know then that one casual glance would be the beginning of a never-ending cataclysm of love.

◆

23rd July 2006

Next day, there was no maths class. Whatever happened that day, it was delectable.

I was not much bothered. So, without much tension, I got ready for the next maths class. Unfortunately, we got the seat in the same second bench, just behind the girls' bench. Sometime later, the girls started entering the room. Ashima and her friends, Divya and Pavitra, couldn't get a seat at their regular bench. So, a friend of theirs called them over to sit on the first bench. I saw them coming and tried to hide myself so that they couldn't spot me behind them. I was busy talking with Firoz, who was on my right. Ashima sat at the end of the bench, near the balcony gate, Divya settled beside her, followed by Pavitra and her unknown friend. I was right behind Pavitra.

Everyone was busy talking, including me. I heard someone whisper from the front bench. "Ask his name. No, I won't. You ask." But I didn't pay much attention.

"What is your name?" Divya suddenly turned around and asked, looking straight at me.

"Aarush Ranjan," I replied in a timid tone. I soon understood that Divya really had nothing to do with my name, because when I looked over at Ashima, I saw that she was giggling, her face in her palms.

"Why don't you ask her why she actually wanted to know your name?" Firoz said, sounding amazed and bewildered.

"Yes, I should ..." I mumbled

"Excuse me," I called in such a hushed tone that no one heard it except me. Both the girls were busy laughing and talking. I left it there.

Sir entered the class and, as usual, he strolled into the balcony as his phone rang.

"Where do you stay?" It was Ashima this time, with a soft voice and a smiling face. "Where are you from?"

I was discussing something with Firoz. And this question simply broke all my concentration.

Really, there was something arresting about her, which tantalized my nerves. A sweet feeling. Something very different. I was sensing this unusual feeling for the first time ever. And it was the first time I ever saw her so closely too. My eyes lingered on her face. She was somewhat oval-faced with fair complexion and a pair of sexy, attentive and attractive, big hazel eyes, decorated with two slender, bow-like eyebrows. Her thick, dark black eyebrows were knitted together, giving a perfect contrast to her complexion; a mouth adorned with two pinkish full lips, black silky hair – her hair looked like it was never disarranged, and it glared brown, may be, due to sun rays falling directly on her; a nose jutting out sharply. Overall, her face was prepossessing. Her voice was really soft and sweet like honey. She appeared cute and beautiful.

"Where do you live?" she asked again in her pleasing voice. "In an out-house?"

"No, I live in a flat with my seniors and friends. And I am from Siwan," I said, wiping my forehead that was sweating profusely by then.

"Where is it? Are you from Patna?" she asked quizzically.

"No, it is in Bihar, but about four hours from Patna," I said quickly. Manav and Mayank were more than puzzled, curious to know what was going on as we talked. I really wanted to stop this chat, though I felt greatly happy deep inside. God heard me and sir bustled into room; she instantly turned around towards the board again.

There were no more conversations after that.

◆

28th July 2006

After this, I started waiting for the maths class eagerly, which took place on alternate days in a week. That day, I wore gray coloured pants and a white shirt with red stripes. I couldn't express my feelings towards this girl to anyone, because they would simply mock me. I had also developed a sneaking affection towards her. I went to the class fifteen minutes earlier, so that I could see her. She was there with her friends. I too started a little chat with my friends, though every now and then, I continued to glimpse over at her. Again in the class, I took the same seat and Ashima took hers on the bench right in front of mine.

She turned back and said, "Where did you rush off so quickly the other day? And don't go away after the tuition. Just wait downstairs. I need to have a word with you."

I was surprised at the way she spoke so frankly. After a minute's hesitation, I finally uttered in a low tone, "Umm... okay. I will be there."

She didn't speak a single word after that during the class. Her long, silky hair was falling over her shoulders. I wasn't able to take my eyes off her back. She was so attractive and charming. The most noticeable aspect was that she herself had approached me. I was relentlessly staring at her though I could get only the side view of her face.

When the class finally dispersed, I rushed down and waited for her near the bicycle stand while my friends stood at a nearby sweet shop where I had asked them to wait for a few minutes. She came over with her friends, looked around for a moment and, finally spotting me, started walking in my direction. As she approached, my forehead was covered in sweat again. I wiped it off without acknowledging her.

Many boys had already started gaping at us. Their stares wasn't looking good. Finally, she appeared, halting a foot away from me. I was standing silently with my hands clasped.

She wore her school uniform that day; she might have come directly from the school. A white shirt, a badge pinned on the pocket, and a nicely pleated white skirt touching her knees.

"Hello, I am Ashima," she said softly, giving out her hand for a friendly shake. "I want to be your friend. Friends?"

I reciprocated the same by shaking her hand and stayed calm, staring at the floor. My head was demurely lowered.

"Nice shirt there!"

I could only nod.

"Do you want to be my friend?" she asked again softly.

I was sweating again. I didn't know what to do as I was evidently anxious to stop the conversation. "My friends are waiting for me. Take my number. I will talk to you later. Have to go," I said slowly. She hurriedly took out a pen from her bag to note down my number on her palm. She seemed to be smiling forever. She said that she would call me in the evening.

"Why do you look down all the time?" she said, rearranging her hair strands that were hanging limply over her forehead. That day, her hair looked like it was carelessly done, though it was as shiny as ever. It seemed like she had dragged it off her forehead and tied it into a knot in a hurry. Her voice was soft, soothing and smiling. A saccharine smile.

"Umm, just like that," I said, looking up at her. Every now and then, I raised my eyes to look at her. What I could see in her eyes was a sparkling joy. But I was sweating profoundly.

"Why are you sweating?"

I didn't say anything and started wiping my forehead hastily.

"You seem to be very shy. Shyness is unheard of in men. But, looking at you, I think that's wrong," she said with a wide smile. "By the way, what's your score? And which school are you in?"

No shyness in girls amazes me, I thought.

She smiled a great deal, and when she smiled, she tried to hide her teeth as two of her teeth overlapped. That day, she seemed to have put on some bit of make-up too.

"91%. I am in Chinmaya, Computer section," I said murmuring.

"Congratulations. I am in DPS, Economics section," she said. "You are very handsome. Your spectacles and hairstyle are awesome." The last sentences were quite abrupt and least expected.

And then, I knew I couldn't continue this conversation anymore. "Now, I have to go," I said, without responding to her compliment. I strolled towards the sweet shop. I didn't turn to see her reaction. I was so nervous that I did not notice her flowery adolescence.

All my friends were smiling and shouting. A bunch of questions hit me – what she had asked me and what I had said in response. I briefed them about our conversation.

Instead of leaving for the hostel, we roamed within those premises as we had our Chemistry tuition next. In the middle of the class, I got a call. I cancelled it and checked the number; it was an unknown contact. Realizing that she was calling me, I felt really glad deep inside and eagerly waited for the class to end. After an hour, the class was finally over.

Firoz was saying something, but I wasn't really listening. My mind was already wandering over her thoughts and her call. My phone started vibrating again. I checked the number; the same unknown contact.

The class had just ended, and I drove myself out of the class as fast as I could without looking back to check if Firoz was accompanying me. The moment I was out of the building, I pulled out my mobile, redialled the number, and gave a missed call, moving at a slower pace now. A few seconds later, my phone started ringing again. More delighted than ever, I answered the call.

"Hello," I said slowly, trying to sound sweet and soft.

"Hello, Aarush ..." answered a honeyed voice. It felt like someone was decanting honey into my ear. A sweet feeling.

"Yes, who is this?" I asked though I knew who the caller was. I felt an excitement, but it vanished soon.

"Ashima here. Actually, there are people around here in my house. So, I will call you later, if you don't mind," she continued.

"Okay," I said as the call ended. Firoz soon joined me and we walked towards the hostel.

5

Evens a day's gap made me impatient. I didn't get a call that day, one of the reasons for me to worry. I waited for the next day and tried to concentrate on my studies. In the evening, Firoz came over to ask what I had planned about the physics tuition. After enquiring from our seniors, we joined Surender Singh's class on Tuesday in the alternate batch.

I went to the school promptly in time and took my seat on the last bench as usual. Again, that day, it was Shubhashish who sat beside me, like he usually did in the other physics classes. I had come to know that he was a Bengali and had joined FIIT JEE, a coaching institute for IIT JEE. A great deal of fuss had been going on about the IIT JEE course. Next, it was the period of our class teacher who taught us Computer Science, 'Mr Golu', a nickname given to him by the old students. His name was Mr Neelanjan Choudhary. Most importantly, this comical name perfectly suited his personality as he was of medium height, with almost no hair on his head, had his belly bulging out, his pants belted all the way below his belly. When he laughed, his whole belly jiggled like jelly.

He announced loudly, "The first mid-term exam will be held from 4th of August and the syllabus for the Computer Section is the first chapter and the half of the next."

The next day, I dressed up quickly and got ready for the maths tuition. We reached the class at ten minutes to four in the evening. We thought that we were late, but all the students were still waiting on the ground floor. I understood that the previous class wasn't done yet.

Ashima wasn't around. All her friends could be seen, except Divya. I was a little surprised at this. Sometime later, she arrived with Divya on a light green scooty. Every time I saw her, I was hit with thoughts like how beautiful she was, and how a girl such as her had come over and spoken to me. A smile swiftly crossed my lips when we saw each other. .

Even on that day, unfortunately or fortunately, we got the same seats in the class. This time everyone was very interested about us. So, they started shooting puzzled looks right from the start of the class.

She turned back and said affably, "Can you wait for me for a few minutes downstairs?"

I nodded.

"I want to talk to you. So, please don't run away."

I was intently listening to her, watching her pinkish lips, parting slightly each time to thrust out the words with subtle cadence. She said, "Then, wait for me!"

"Yes," I stammered and nodded.

After the class ended, I stood near the passage at the corner with my friends as I had already informed them about this meeting while creeping downstairs.

She came a few minutes later along with her friends. She saw me and smiled. After a brief talk, her friends left her and rushed away towards the parking area. I was nervous and shaking.

She strolled towards me smiling and stopped a meter away, right before me. Her friends were still laughing; instead of going over to the parking lot, they just stood there, watching intently what was going on. This was making me even more nervous. Her gestures made me realize that she was there. I signaled to my friends to wait for me.

"Hi," she said.

I replied the same, as sweetly and softly as I could.

"Where do you go so quickly after the class every day?" she said with an inquiring voice.

"Nowhere … I go to the hostel. Fast? No, I always go slowly and I don't even have a cycle," I stammered as I hadn't expected such a question.

"But I never see you. Are you a magician? Just waving a wand and thrusting some spells and vanishing," she said with a little laugh.

She was looking so beautiful that I couldn't measure it at that moment. Her way of talking, her friendly manner, the movement of her shiny eyes, the parting of her fluffy lips, gestures of her hands. They all made me nervous while answering. When you have such a beautiful girl standing in front of you, it turns out to be really difficult not to get tense.

I didn't say much and, before we could leave the place, Manav came over to us and said, "Tomorrow is Aarush's birthday."

She looked at me for confirmation. I nodded. Manav whispered in my ear, asking me to start for the hostel. I waved her bye and turned back to join them. Suddenly, she too raised her head and our eyes met. A miniscule smile was left on both our lips. I liked this, but there was a problem which was gnawing inside me for a long time.

◆

The next day was a very hot oune; the sun was hovering above like a launching fire ball. The acclivity of the road resulted in more sweating and wastage of energy.

Firoz reached the hostel earlier by making an excuse of having a stomach ache and came back from the class an hour earlier.

I opened my lunch box when Firoz suddenly asked, "So, has anyone wished you?" He came over to me.

"No, no one," I said. "No one knows it's my birthday in class."

"I am going to Aftab bhaiya's room," he said. "Come after lunch." And he readily left the room with a bang on the door.

After finishing my lunch, I abandoned the idea of going to Aftab bhaiya's room and lay down on the bed. It was half past one when my phone rang. I picked it up from my bed and glanced over at the number. It was an unknown one. Surprised, I picked up the phone.

"Hello," I said calmly.

"Hello, Aarush?" A girl was on the other side. I was surprised even more, now.

"Yes, who is this?" I tried to sound as polite as possible.

"I am Divya, Ashima's friend. You might know me. By the way, happy birthday," she said.

"How would I not know you? Thanks," I said affably.

"Well, some relatives are visiting her. So, she told me to inform you that she might call you later." She completed her statement without a break, in one sentence.

I was relieved and said okay, and she hung up the call, after the formal good bye.

I placed the phone back at the same place and repositioned myself to sleep again. I pulled my thin sheet up to my chin.

A few minutes later, my phone rang again. Another unknown number. I thought for a while and picked up the phone.

"Hello," I said.

"Hello, I am Ashima. Happy birthday. Many many happy returns of the day," she said hurriedly though she sounded very sweet.

"Thanks," I replied joyfully. "Divya called a few minutes ago to inform me about you."

"Ok ... Yeah, some relatives have come. Don't call me on this number. I will call you later. I am in a great hurry now, as I have sneaked into the bathroom to call you secretly," she said hurriedly as her mummy started calling her.

"Okay bye," I said half-heartedly as the phone went dead. This little conversation left a smile on my face. I was really very happy.

After the physics tuition, we went over to the city centre and brought some, samosas, biscuits, cold drinks, and sweets.

We enjoyed a lot that night. We danced like kids to popular Hindi songs. Firoz had managed to arrange woofers and speakers. It was really a great day for me, having fun with my best friends. We slept late that night, me feeling happier than ever.

6

30th July 2006

Next day when we returned from tuition around 8:00 p.m., there was no sign of anyone in the rooms. The lights were switched off too, with only a bulb lit giving a very dim, yellow light in the hall. "Maybe they are on the roof," I thought.

On the contrary, they were all gathered in our room, near Firoz's bed. Aftab bhaiya and Avinash bhaiya were seated silently on Firoz's bed. Ritesh and Aditya bhaiya were standing near Manav's bed, and both were engaged in a conversation. As we entered the room, suddenly, everyone went quiet. There was utter silence. No one spoke. I didn't have the strength to ask anything. I didn't dare.

"Oh, everyone is here. We thought you are on the roof," Firoz said with a smile.

I still was unable to understand what was going on. I was paranoid as all of them were staring at me, without blinking their eyes even once.

"Who was she?"Aftab asked in a deep and harsh tone, looking directly at me.

I said in dismay, "She is Ashima and she came to talk to me."

Everyone was silent and had a sharp gaze at my face.

"I'm afraid she is Ashima Ram," Aftab bhaiya said with a sharp gaze at me. He was stern in his tone, "We know her. We enquired about her with a friend from DPS. She is not a good girl. Already she has had too many boyfriends. She is a flirt, so it is better to tell her that you won't talk to her any longer. She has spoilt the lives of many boys till now."

I was shocked to hear that. A wave of fear swirled in my body. I managed to find myself a seat on the nearby chair. I was very afraid of fights and these kinds of girls. I didn't believe it at first, but I had to.

This left a rage of tension within me. I was dumbfounded. The result was a pain that choked up my throat.

"I'll not talk to her." This was the best answer at that time, I guess. "I will tell her that I can't talk to her." Everyone rose up and walked out of the room. Except the three of us – the roommates.

There was a short uneasy calmness that swooped across the room after they had left. No one uttered a word.

I had no idea of how this information went up to the seniors. Who could have leaked it, I wondered.

Firoz's words broke the silence, "Aarush, what do you think about this?"

I gestured him to come outside the room. We headed towards the empty balcony, silently and swiftly.

"There is nothing to think here," I said. "I will refuse her proposal. I don't want to take on any trouble."

The next day, she was still in the classroom though the class was over. That day, many students were still in the campus. Few of them were on bikes. They had an ugly attitude. I understood the situation; it seemed that they were there for me. A mob gathered around the building. I was with my friends. So to avoid this, we took the passage way. Mayank and Manav drifted a few yards ahead, leaving Firoz and me near her. We both walked towards Ashima.

I was silent. Firoz said in a deep tone "Sorry, we cannot talk to you. We are here to study. We don't want to indulge in all this. Please don't take it in any wrong sense."

I shook my head, my face was reflecting a shadow of sadness. Firoz left after this.

I was still silent. My face shrunk, and then I heard some hooting from the back, from the same ugly boys. "*Le le.* See those love birds. See them."

A boy, with an ugly face and dirty oiled hair passed near Ashima and said in a very rough tone pointing at me, "Why him? I am far better than him. My proposal is still open for you."

Her eyes glinted with fury. Same happened with mine too.

"First look at your face in the mirror. And go away. Otherwise your proposal will get my slippers," she hissed.

He fled, mocking her words.

She turned back to me, remained silent for a moment, in a deep thought, and said, "Okay, forget about this friendship."

It seemed that she was sad and her words revealed her disappointment.

"Okay, nice talking to you," she smiled and turned back.

Her face wasn't pinkish that day. Her smile wasn't the same as it used to be when she saw me. I was sad and low too. Leaving this aside, we also turned back. I drifted towards Mayank and Manav who were waiting for us near at the sweet shop.

The group of boys was looking at us suspiciously. One of them was Deependra. He was fat and tall, and sitting on a bike. I had heard about him that he was also one of those self-decided lovers of Ashima and had been madly chasing her. And another boy, standing beside him, was Himanshu.

We were still walking towards the sweet shop when someone shouted from behind. I moved ahead ignoring it. But the second time, the shout was a little louder than before.

"Hey, gray t-shirt!" someone said loudly.

This made me stop. I was wearing a gray t-shirt that day. I turned back.

A boy on the bike pointed at me and signaled at me to come to him. I didn't know him. We understood the situation. Mayank patted me and signaled me not to worry, but to go ahead. Mayank instructed the rest to wait there.

As we both moved ahead, Ashima rushed towards me and said, "Aarush, don't go there, please!"

Fear flickered across her face – a wan and strained fear. She was frightened. I tried to remain silent and patient. I tried not to show my fear.

I signaled to her not to worry and gestured to her to stop. "Nothing will happen."

We walked towards them. When we reached there, the same boy on the Pulsar bike laughed cheaply.. He was mocking us.

Mayank was silent. We waited for any unnatural moves by them. I gave a sharp look to Deependra, just to see what he was doing at that time. He came near the boy on the bike, and said something. I didn't know what he told him as he spoke a different language.

It was very depressing. I could sense a hint of fear, though nothing strange happened.

We stood there for a few moments and I turned back.

All those incidents had brought a bad feeling. I was sad, since it was my last conversation with her. But on the other hand, I thought it was good that I was out of this situation.

I tried to remain calm and normal, and tried to put my mind on other things.

A couple of days later, an attendant brought a notice about the mid-term examinations. There were about to start in four more days. So, I started putting my effort into my studies.

But I heard a girl speaking something unusual about me and Ashima in the classroom at the time of recess. The rumour spread faster than a forest fire.

The examinations started and ended too. The results were not at all good – a complete opposite of what it used to be in my school. It was very bad, beyond my imagination. I hadn't got such marks ever till the tenth grade. I didn't know that this was the beginning of my end.

7

Deependra wasn't coming to the tuitions, not even Himanshu, the two self-claimed lovers of Ashima. But she was regular in class. I initially didn't pay much attention towards her. Everything was going normally.

With the passing days, one thing I noticed about myself was that I found myself thinking about her with more frequency and interest than I cared to allow. I even asked myself in great distress, why it was happening. I thought about her more for sure. I could have never imagined thinking about anyone like this. I used to frequently steal glances to see where she was. In class, I gazed at her beautiful face the whole time. I really liked her smile and long black eyelashes.

14th August 2006

That day, I had my mathematics class. I reached in time along with Manav. The sun weaved the ephemeral shades of pink and orange through the sky. There was a gentle breeze through the air, creating a romantic atmosphere.

I was looking for her. For some time, I couldn't get sight of her. I came to Natkhat Sweets so that I could see her scooty from a distance.

After some time, she appeared along with Pavitra and Divya. She wore a dark red suit, embroidered with golden thread. That suited her well and she was looking like a doll – even better than a Barbie doll. Her hair was done up properly and was shining. I glanced over at her. She looked at me. I smiled. She reciprocated with a very warm smile. There was something in her smile that fueled my instinct; I was sure she was going to call me. Whatever it might be, I was happy. And I turned towards the staircase.

Firoz and thr others reached just a minute before the class began. In class, we exchanged smiles thrice. Every time she smiled, it led me to think that she was going to call.

After coming back at around 5:30, I went outside. By mistake, I had left my mobile on the window sill.

I freshened up and came into the room. I took my phone. It was my habit to check my mobile every now and then to confirm whether there were any messages or missed calls.

There were five missed calls. I checked the number enthusiastically with a sudden surge of unease. My heart gave a somersault. It was Ashima. She had called me five times. Why, I didn't know. I was quite excited and happy. Because after that incident, I had lost all hope that I would ever talk to her.

I cursed myself for not carrying my phone with me and losing the golden chance. Since she had called me two minutes earlier, I thought she might be there, so I called back and left a missed call on her landline number.

I marched into the hall with the phone in my hand, waiting enthusiastically to talk to her after a long time.

After a few minutes, my mobile rang. I was happy. But I didn't know what I would talk to her about. Then I thought that I'd ask why she had called me. A moment later, I answered the call.

"Hello," I said.

"Hello," The reply was much softer.

"You had called me some time back. Sorry I couldn't pick up the phone," I said trying to be polite.

"Yes, I called to tell you to warn Firoz not to spread any rumours about me," she said.

I thought for a while about what he might have done. "Now, what has he done? Really, I don't know," I said in disbelief. My mood swung from happiness to a bit of tension.

She soon averted the issue and started saying that she didn't like Firoz's statement that we came here to study and we don't want to get ourselves in trouble.

I tried to recall when that had happened, but I said nothing.

"What does he mean by saying 'I'm not here to enjoy?' Am I here to enjoy?" she continued. Her voice was filled with frustration and anger.

I said sorry on Firoz's behalf.

Silence. A very long silence followed. Her voice broke after a moment of silence which was filled with uneasiness.

"Why did you reject my proposal?" she said. "Am I not beautiful?" she continued and tried to ingratiate herself, speaking sweetly.

"No, it's not like that. All I can say that you are..." I said. "You are... I mean you are very beautiful and sexy too." The world 'sexy' just slipped from my mouth.

There was silence on the other side. I too, fell silent.

"Oh, what did I say?" I thought. "What will she think about me?" It was obvious that I had made a terrible impression upon her.

After a moment, she said, "Then why did you reject my proposal?"

I said, after a brief pause, "Actually, you are a quite different; you are so bold and frank. I always hoped for a sweet and simple girl."

"Hmm. But there must be something as you cannot take your eyes off me."

I felt shy. I didn't know what to answer. "No no... I... I never stared at you. Why... why'd I stare at you?" I stammered as I hadn't expected this question.

"Oh, you do. I know very well." Her tone was becoming very familiar as if I had known her for longer now. "You always steal glances at me. Always wait passionately for me."

We were silent for a minute. An unexpected, astonishing phrase broke the silence and unsettled me.

"Aarush, I love you. I will make myself as you wish – sweet and lovely. Simple too," she said suddenly. It stunned me. It was not the response which I expected from her, at least not this time or so early. I could not believe what she had said.

"What?" I said in disbelief, still not believing what I had heard a few seconds earlier. I stood puzzled wondering what if I had heard was right, or was I imagining it all? Her words left me baffled, and I had to struggle to talk.

It was going to be one of the most difficult time, and maybe the most exciting time of my life. Both of us were silent. I was speechless. I had not dreamt that this would happen. Even if it did, then not this soon.

"Do you know what you are saying?" I told her, to make her realize what she said a minute earlier. "You hardly know me, we don't know each other. In fact, we have met just one month earlier. You know nothing about me – my behavior, my background. How could you say these words so casually?"

"Aarush, I know what you are saying. But I don't want to know about your past. I know that you are not a bad person. To fall in love with someone, it's not quite necessary to find his background. I found a sweet, lovable nature in you, and that made me fall in love with you. Anyhow, I know a little about you. I got to know more about you from my friend, and only after have I told you my feelings," she said in a stern tone.

This left me even more surprised. I had come here two months earlier and people seemed to know everything about me. I didn't know anything about her and not so much even about my roommate. The girl I barely knew, knew everything about me. I was surprised.

"But do you think you can call it love? You have seen me for a while; we have talked very little. In other words, you have fallen in love with me after just a short meeting?" I asked with curiosity.

"Yes, I'm in love with you madly. I'm in love with you from the very first sight. I found you very sweet. How you felt shy seeing me, talking to me. Your face blushed red. It was really so sweet and cute. In fact, anyone can fall in love with you seeing your decency, innocence and moreover, your smile is the best thing I have ever seen in my life. Am I not correct about you?"

I was drowned in deep thoughts and came out in front of a mirror. I tried to smile, but couldn't do so. Then, one more sentence broke my attention and it seemed like America had dropped an atom bomb over Nagasaki and Hiroshima once again.

"Do you love me?" she asked in a deep tone.

"I don't know," I said. "But we can be friends."

We were silent. It lasted for a minute before her soothing voice broke the silence.

"Can we talk on the phone?" she asked.

I thought for a while and said, "Yes." Hearing this, I sensed her happiness in her giggling. I also did not want to lose her and this could have been my last chance. I was happy inside.

"But there is a problem." My happiness turned into sweat over my forehead, thinking about the seniors and the situation I had faced.

"What? Is something bothering you?"

"We are talking on phone and will continue to do so. No one should know about this otherwise it will be a problem for us both," I said.

"Both? I don't understand what you meant by the both. I can understand one is seniors but..."

"What about that fat, tall boy who had come that day?" I started before she completed her sentence.

"Don't worry about him. He is in my school. I had already scolded him, and warned that if anything happens, then my slippers across his mouth is what he will face!" she said with unusual fervor.

"Okay, I have to hang up now. My mother is calling me," I said.

"I love you," she said. It sounded sweet. She held the phone still on line for a moment. Maybe she was waiting for my reply, but I didn't utter a single word. And the phone went dead after a "Bye".

I came back into the room. Nobody else had come yet. I sat down, thinking about the call.

"Is it a dream?" I pinched myself to confirm it; no it was not one. But how had it happened so early? It happens on television soaps, but it had happened in my life now. Wow!

I was in euphoria all day. I slipped into a nap thinking of her.

A noise broke my dream as everyone had returned. I sat on the bed. They all were in Aftab bhaiya's room. I pushed the door shut and remained in my room, awake and trying to concentrate on my studies. But I was not successful. Those three words, 'I love you' echoed in my mind.

Earlier, I used to keep my phone here and there. Now, I started carrying my phone along with myself. I also locked my phone. I didn't want anyone to know about this.

8

Every thing was going as usual. We went to the tuition classes, exchanged a few smiles – sweet and innocent ones without being noticed by anyone. Foreseeing all kinds of difficulties, I decided to pass a message of my affection in code language – an indispensible strategy for forbidden love – that I had read somewhere in some magazine. I always cast a furtive glance at her, while in class or outside. And whenever I saw her, I would dissolve into measuring the contour of her radiant face, her beauty and her smile. I would gaze straight into her eyes and study her face carefully. But in the classroom, these looks of mine never could last longer than ten to fifteen seconds. My hardest attempt persisted for half a minute before she turned back and saw me and smiled coyly in a way that embarrassed me. Sometimes the intensity, determination, and love visible in my eyes would make her smile, a hint of a smile that would not leave her lips easily.

She used to call me in the evening, sometimes before dinner, and we would talk for a while. I always wished that our conversation would continue for longer – maybe forever. She always waited at the time of hanging the phone, after saying a sweet 'I love you', for me to say something. But I never said anything and a short silence used to follow before I'd finally put the phone down.

As days passed, I became more and more fond of her. Those sly looks, reciprocating saccharine smiles, giggles at sir's jokes, looking with those besotting eyes without blinking, devouring the note of love, passing unwritten, undefined message of love and affection from her had become the essence of the maths tuition. But I had not said those words to her yet. And I was unaware that I was going to soon.

4th September 2006

It was around 9:00 p.m. when I entered my room after dinner. I pushed the door and saw two figures that were jubilantly swaying with each other on my bed.

"Firoz, is this you?" I asked as I was surprised about what they were doing.

"Yeah! But not alone. Aditya bhaiya is also here, beside me!" Firoz took his head out of the sheets and said. "Not beside… above me."

"What is Aditya bhaiya doing here? Wait...Wait...Wait... What are both of you doing?" I said. So, Aditya came out of the sheet and smirked.

"We are sleeping," Firoz said.

"Together?" I got more surprised.

"Yeah! Any problem?" Firoz said.

"Why should I? But with a boy?"

"Why? Why can't I?" Firoz tried his best to defend himself. "Moreover, it is very common everywhere."

"You mean you are gay?" My eyes widened listening to his words.

"Not exactly."

"Then, what? And come out of my bed," I said angrily.

Without any argument, both came out looking at each other. They both were in their underwear.

"What is this? You were in your underwear?" I asked. "Firoz, why are you forgetting that you were straight in class tenth. What happened to you now?"

He didn't say anything and both of them went out of the room.

It was 10:30 p.m. when I slipped into bed. I was feeling drowsy as I was an early sleeper. Firoz was busy with something. I didn't care about it and pulled the sheet till my forehead.

Fifteen minutes later.

"Aarush, your phone is ringing," Firoz shouted. But I didn't wake up. He came near me and forced me and handed me my phone. It seemed blurred to me. I dragged my spectacles. It was an unknown number.

"Hello," I said in a low voice, sounding dull. I was not completely awake, after all.

"Hello." A sweet sound came from the other side.

I immediately recognized the sound on the other side of the line. Ashima. A smile automatically fluttered across my face, and the dullness vanished.

"Hi, what are you doing?" she asked in a voice was full of confidence.

"Hi, I didn't expect your call at this time," I replied. "I was just on my bed," I said slowly. A continuous smile was flowing across my lips, and I was rubbing my eyes with one hand. "Whose number is this?" I asked.

"How sweet, my boyfriend doesn't know how to lie. It is my dad's phone. Actually, I am leaving for Kanpur tomorrow. So, I called you to inform that I will be not able to call you for three days," she said. Her voice sounded a bit low.

"Kanpur? Are there any relatives of yours?" I asked curiously. "But there is no festival now. Raksha bandhan is also over."

She first giggled and said, "My sister is studying there. So we are going to meet her."

"Which college?"

"IIT Kanpur."

I became silent for a minute. "IIT Kanpur, IIT Kanpur," I whispered twice, realizing how big this was. IIT was a dream for every Science student; for me too. Few months ago, I didn't even know the name of IIT. But after coming to Bokaro, I learned the hullaballoo over IIT and I also jumped into the rat race. But this was the first time that I came to know of any IITian.

"I will come after three days. I will try to call you from there," she continued.

I had nothing to say except "Ok". I didn't want her go anywhere. I didn't want to pass a single day without talking to her. But I felt utterly helpless. I tried to control my feelings as I hadn't said "I love you" to her yet.

"Can we talk in the night?" I asked.

"Ok," she said after a few seconds. "But until I call, don't call me."

"Ok, sounds good," I said, controlling my happiness. "So when are you leaving tomorrow?"

"Tomorrow morning, at around at 6 o'clock."

"So, going with your mom and dad? Is your brother also going along?" I asked. She has a brother, younger to her and her sister. He was also in DPS.

"No."

"Okay, I need to hang up now. I have to pack my bag," she continued.

I didn't want to hang up yet, and hoped this conversation to continue forever, but—

"Bye," she said.

"Okay bye, take care of yourself. Have a nice journey," I said glumly. "And please try to call me from there."

"Wait..." she said. "I love you."

She paused. She was waiting for me to speak. I wondered that I would say something. I knew that she wanted me to tell her that I loved her. I loved her too, but I didn't utter a word.

"Okay, bye. Take care," she said as her voice grew slower. And then, the phone went dead.

I stretched on the bed, pulling the sheet up to my forehead.

◆

It was really a good night. But the coming two days seemed to turn into bad, withering, rough days without her calls. The deadly wait brought a feeling of uneasiness, flooding my heart with her absence. Waiting was a torture; I had never felt like this before.

A pain. A deadly pain. A deadly wait.

"What Aarush, what happened to you? Waiting impatiently for a call? Her smile brings a smile on your face. You wait impatiently to see her, to attend her call. What is happening to you? You have fallen in love with her. Is this what people call love?" I asked myself. I was afraid to feel this, to realize that I had fallen in love. This thought and pang of sweet anxiety rushed within me.

For a few weeks, I noticed that my heart started to pound whenever she called me. I impatiently waited for her call. I wished to talk for longer. Suddenly,I realized that I was in love, in love with her. An invisible force had made me fall madly in love with her. I thought I should also say those words to her. *'I love you'* which I should have said much earlier. But how would I initiate? It had been a long time. I was brooding over that. Then, I decided to write my feelings on a paper, but did not intend to pass the same to her. I wrote many pages of my feelings, and soon I had a thick bundle of papers. I read it many times. Sometimes, it pleased me very much. By the time she arrived, it included ten long pages of a diary written on both sides. I didn't even know how many times I edited it, rewrote it to make it more meaningful. Finally, I had put my heart on paper through words.

Finally, I decided to say those lovely words to her after rehearsing it so many times, sometimes in front of a mirror and sometimes on the roof. I practiced my facial expressions to make it sweet. Though, later, I realized my foolishness and laughed at myself. No one looked at each other on the phone.

◆

6th September 2006

The teachers announced that the first term examination would begin from 8th September. They marked the syllabi in their respective subjects. A demon was on its way to ride over us. Everyone was looking tensed, except a few, studious ones. In the evening, I got a call from her from her sister's mobile.

"Hi, when did you reach?" I asked.

"In the morning, how are you? What were you doing? Are you missing me?" she asked a series of question more dangerous than America's missile attack on the Taliban, Nevertheless, it sounded very nice. When someone cares for you, it feels amazing. I always hoped that someone would care for me. And I was experiencing it now.

"Nothing much, just reading the newspaper," I replied. And I didn't answer the 'missing' question deliberately.

"Aren't you missing me?" she repeated it. Girls always wait for an answer to such questions.

"No, why should I?" I teased in a serious tone.

"Really! You aren't missing me?" She was hopeful, and her voice grew sad.

"Ashima!" I said calmly because I know that I couldn't see her like this.

"What now? I hope you are not going to say I love you to me."

"*I love you.*"

"What?" Her voice pumped out suddenly. "Say it again. I must be dreaming? Aarush, am I dreaming? Please tell me…"

"*I love you.*"

I was also surprised at how easily it came out.

"But how?" she was almost astonished. She was silent.

"Maybe your absence made me realize that I love you. Maybe I am missing you too much. Your hair over your face, smile on your lips, your big intoxicating eyes. I miss all these things. People are right about the fact that sometimes the absence of loved ones makes you realize their importance. I think it happened for me too. I love you, I love you very much."

First, she remained silent with disbelief. I knew what she was thinking – what would happen if my seniors came to know about this. A silence followed before she said, "But Aarush..."

"I know what you want to say," I added in the same tone.

Her silence assured me. I had guessed it right.

"Ashima, I know you love me. I also started loving you the day you said 'I love you' to me. I also wished to say this to you, but the fear of my seniors made me keep quiet. It has been a month since I've been talking to you. You always say '*I love you*' to me. Now, I can't keep this within me. Those three lovely and sweet words have been stirring within me for a month. How many times have you waited to hear these beautiful words, I know. How long you might have uttered them in your dreams! I even know how many times you might have said to your friends with excitement about the two of us... how you found and met me. You need not worry. Nothing will happen. We will keep this a secret," I said, keeping my tone filled with sweetness and firmness. "We will keep our relationship hidden."

She listened and said, "Aarush, I feel lucky that you are my boyfriend. I am really proud of myself that my love loves me a lot. You can't imagine how happy I am now. You think so much for me, for our relationship. I really love you."

"I love you too."

She asked me to say it again and again. There was no kidding this time as she sensed my serious and deep tone filled with sweetness and firmness.

"*I love you.*" Each time, my voice was growing louder with a sense of deep calmness.

She barely could contain her happiness which I could easily sense. It took an effort to not shriek with joy as she had done.

"I miss you very much," I finally told her.

"Oh, I miss you too," she said, her voice full of excitement, a joyous time for her. Her voice was revealing her excitement as she became breathless with joy. "I will be back soon, now I need to hang up. Don't call on this number. I love you; bye and please say those words again."

First I laughed and then said, "I love you". She hung up after this.

Soon after disconnecting the phone, it looked like I had crashed. And I was in heaven where everything was filled with only happiness. Every moment was lively and full of love, something I had been searching for throughout my life. My longing for true love was around me. I wanted to catch everything in my eyes; every single sound in my ears, every feeling I wanted to feel. My dream of adoring someone had finally come true. A mist of a positive future started enveloping me.

◆

I never forgot to mention every detail of this love story in my diary. When we met, when she said she loved me, when I said I loved her. Every page in the diary looked identical to what had actually happened. All these entries began with the same words and ended with the same phrase. *I love you*. I decorated the diary. On the first page, I wrote our name in two big hearts, an arrow attaching both. Every feeling, emotion, I was capturing in it.

This time examinations were torturing me; nothing was prepared. Till class tenth, I used to prepare every subject well before exams, but this time, everything was reversed. Even Firoz was looking serious and started turning pages after pages. As usual, Manav was studying hard. His exams were about to start one day before ours.

I started one by one; practicing maths, practicing physics, clearing concepts, and mugging up chemistry.

Finally, the battle had started. She had arrived in Bokaro. I didn't inform her about the exams; time had elapsed in those lovely talks. I came at 1 p.m. A message flashed on my screen. I hurriedly opened it, hoping it might be hers as there was no message or a call the previous day from her. I was correct:

"Back to Bokaro.

Call you later. ILY"

A smile fluttered across my lips and halfheartedly, I deleted the message.

After lunch, I came to bed and opened a thick book in front and started turning pages, like picking a drop from the sea, and it seemed it was never going to end. Till evening, I had completed two units; four units were to be completed for the examination.

I came on the roof for an evening walk, a good time to refresh myself. Wind was blowing gently. But soon I rushed downstairs to my room to take my phone. It was ringing. As I picked the phone and was about to press the receive call button, the phone got disconnected. Three missed calls, I saw. I cursed myself and gave a missed call. She called back.

"Hello."

"Hi, how are you?"

"Fine, my exams are going on, and today was the first. I was studying for next. I got your message," I replied.

"I also came to know today that my exams are going to start after three days," she said.

"Anyway, how was your the trip? How is your sister?"

"She is good, and the trip was good too, but it became wonderful and memorable when you said..." she said and giggled.

"I was really missing you," I said.

"Oh, so sweet, me too," she teased. "I bought a suit there."

"You went there to meet your sister or to buy clothes?" I asked, smiling at her cuteness.

"That's what my mother said to me, but you know that I am fond of new dresses. I always wanted a new blue dress," she said. Her tone was mixed with calmness and sweetness. "Oh, I forgot to ask how your exam was."

"*Aah*, you remember now! It was fine," I tried to tease, controlling my tone. "I solved every question, except one."

She said she was happy it had gone well. "You know, I have activated my 10 paisa per minute plan on your number, so that our call cost will be cheaper," I said excitedly.

"I don't understand, activated the plan means?"

"Actually, there is a BSNL plan, in which you chose two numbers to call at 10 paisa per minute anytime," I cleared her confusion.

"Oh, it's really great." Her excitement made me happy and I smiled again. "But, call me only when I give you a missed call. I will also activate the same plan," she said.

I teased her that she was a copy cat.

"*Tum kitne gande ho.*"

"*Gande*? What did I do?" I said, amused.

"Oh, I am also teasing you."

"You naughty." And we started laughing together.

"*Tum kitne gande ho*, also sounded so sweet and cute," I said.

"Now, I have to hang up, my mother is coming," she said amidst smiles.

"So soon… it has been only five minutes," I said disappointed.

"No, it has been twenty-five minutes dear. I will call you in the night, then we will talk, bye," she said.

"I love you."

"I love you too." She hung up.

A few seconds later, I again called her. "Hello, I love you."

"So sweet. I love you too," she said, cheerfully

◆

Next few days were hectic and fearful. All of us were busy in mugging up. All the exams went well, except chemistry. Her exams were also about to end one day after our exams, as DPS conducted exams daily; five days and the exams are over! We were hardly talking, only during the night before going to bed, merely to say 'good night and sweet dreams' and 'I love you too.'

"Exams are over, hurray!" Firoz shouted, throwing his bag on the bed. The shout was louder than a Trojan soldier winning a battle.

At night, we went to the movie theatre for a Hollywood action movie. I used to pass my English exams with great difficulty. How was I going to understand an English movie? Anyhow, I made time to ebb away and we returned to the hostel.

Just as I had finished my dinner in Ritesh bhaiya's room, my phone started vibrating. I understood. I quickly packed up my tiffin, said "I am going to my room," and came out.

By the time I washed my hands, the phone got disconnected. I rushed to my room and closed the door.

I called back, phone was coming busy, and thought "Maybe she is calling me". I came out in the balcony. She called again and without wasting a second, I picked up the phone.

"Hi, where have you been? You didn't pick up the phone." Questions were fired on me.

"Oh, sorry. I was eating, I was about to pick up, but it got disconnected. Sorry," I said slowly.

"Oh, don't be sorry."

"How was your exam?" I asked.

"Good, except physics. I just hate physics. Tomorrow is the last exam."

"Tomorrow we have the maths class too, please come in that blue suit of yours." I tried to divert her from the exam topic, as it really sucked. At least with her, I didn't want to discuss it.

"Yeah. But I don't know whether I will look good or not," she said, unsure.

"You look very beautiful and stunning in every dress," I replied slowly yet internally very excited. "Especially in that red suit. I was speechless when I first saw you in that red suit, and I could easily understand why so many boys are after you. In fact, you look more beautiful in ethnic wear." After a brief pause, I continued, "You know Ashima, I love your name. It's so unusual and unique, like mine. First time, when I heard it, I just loved it."

"No, it's bad. It sounds like the name of a submarine. Ashima. My dad named me. I really don't like it. My sister's name is better. Aakriti," she said, opposing me.

"No, it's good. At least better than my name," I said.

"No, your name is good. Aarush. Sweet, innocent and handsome."

"Okay, your name is silly, so silly....."

"No, it's not as silly as you're making it sound. Only a little bit silly."

I laughed at her sweetness which had always filled my heart with love for her.

We talked for ten more minutes. We said 'goodnight' and 'I love you', to each other, as I wanted her to study. I hung up, but not before I wished her best of luck for the exam.

9

She wore a peacock-blue suit with lovely lilac embroidery. She looked beautiful in that. This was the first time I had seen her in that dress. I had just shown her my thumbs up in a tacit way to indicate that she was looking beautiful. Then I looked around to check if anyone was looking at me. She smiled in return. Suddenly, she averted her eyes.

I saw Divya coming. Ashima averted her eyes and started talking to her. I smiled to myself.

We started talking that night. She called me around 10:45 p.m. I skulked to roof. Luckily, no one was there.

"Hello, what were you doing?" I asked, in a low voice.

"Nothing much. Oh, I remember, I was drowned in your memories. How was my dress?" she said sweetly.

"So sweet! Oh. Dress! It looked lovely on you. It seemed that the dress is made only for you. The stone like pearl was perfectly placed at the bottom of the dress, just like the smile on your face. So lovely… the colour of the duppatta added extra charm to your beauty."

"Aarush, how much you praise me! You are so sweet," she said coyly.

We talked for one hour. How did an hour pass, I couldn't even feel. After keeping the phone down, I called her again. "Hello, I love you!"

"So sweet. I love you too," she said with a giggle. "Goodnight. Sweet dreams. And dream of me only."

"No need to say that. You are in my dreams, and in my breath. Good night."

Actually, it was difficult for me to talk to her at night. The seniors were around all the time. If I talked in the balcony, Firoz would ask who I was talking to. I could not go on to the roof; they might search for me if they did not find me in my bed for a long time. So, it was creating a problem for me thoughI wanted to talk to her also.

Till midnight, the seniors used to stay awake. And she gave me a call around 10:30 p.m. I was desperate to talk to her, so I began searching for a safer place, so that I could talk to her for a longer time, maybe for the entire night.

I had found a way to talk to her. What I generally noticed, seniors used to talk either in my room or Ritesh's bhaiya's room and I used to come in Aftab bhaiya's room. There, Manav usually kept studying. I started talking to her in the balcony till midnight, after which Manav went to sleep, and I crept inside the room, informing Avinash bhaiya that I'd sleep on my bed. I used to slip inside the sheets, covering myself up completely, and talked to her very slowly, till 1 a.m.

Then I came to know more about her. She said that she was a Punjabi and added that she was from Delhi, but her father had been working in the Bokaro steel plant for the last twenty years. He had also graduated from IIT, IIT Kanpur; her whole family had studied in IIT Kanpur, and she also wished to go there.

"Don't worry, you also will study there," I interrupted.

She continued that she had been studying in DPS since childhood, her sister and brother, Kanishk as well. This was the main problem in any relationship. You have to keep a profile of every one of her family, mug up the birthdays of her mother, father, even of her pets if she has one. And if you forget anything, then the drama starts.

◆

One night, while talking to Ashima and saying endless 'I love yous', her voice suddenly stopped me and made me worried.

"Sweetie, are you forgetting something?"

"What? Is it your birthday? But this is September, and yours is in January. Still a long time away," I said brooding for some time. I couldn't guess. "I am sorry. I am not able to remember."

"You really don't love me. You don't care for me. Go away, I am angry with you. I will not talk to you," She kept saying this repeatedly. Such behaviour reminds people from time to time about the world's most mysterious species-women. I often wondered why our scientists waste their time in solving ridiculous puzzles of the world, when they have such a mysterious thing in front of them. Maybe even they are also fed up with it.

"Oh, please tell me what is so special today? Sorry sweetie, I am unable to remember."

"It is my mother's birthday."

"Oh god! I don't remember my mother's birthday, how could I remember her mother's birthday?" I thought.

"Oh really, wish her on my behalf," I said.

"No, you are very bad. You really don't care."

"It is not a big deal."

"Not a big deal? How can you say that? She is your prospective mother-in-low." She stumped me.

"Mother-in-law?" I was agape. But when things start turning downhill, I had to answer diplomatically. "Sorry, how can I forget?

Forgive me this time. I am going to stick a reminder for your whole family's dates of birth on my study table after this call."

"No, do it now."

"Okay, hold on," I said and started looking for reminder notes. I didn't have the sticky notes, so I tore a white paper and acted like sticking it up before whispering. "Forgive me, Maa. I don't have even your picture on my table, and I am sticking my prospective mother-in-law's birthday notes."

"And this note is for your father's birthday. 30th November. Last note."

"No, it's not November, it's December."

"I know sweetie. I was just teasing you. Is there someone else left in your family? Oh, I forgot about Tuffy, your dog."

She didn't ask me to leave it, instead she said, "Let me remember. Bobby's birthday is on 5th of December. Oh no, it's on 6th."

"Bobby? Is she your sibling?" I asked.

"No, she is my rabbit."

"Oh god! Why don't you declare that your house is a zoo?" I whispered.

"Aarush!"

"Okay ... I am sorry," I said.

This made her cheer up.

Girls are really foolish. They don't know love should not be in words, but it should be in hearts.

Then, she told me about her best friend, Tulika Bhattacharya. "You know, when I told her about you and about your rejection of my proposal, she was shocked," she said excitedly.

"I don't think there is any reason for this," I said, still thinking for a reason.

"No. Actually a lot of boys are chasing me and have proposed to me, but I never accepted, and you rejected my proposal. That's what she was saying."

Then, she told me about her favourite food: chicken, rajma and chaval. She told me that she was very fond of new dresses, perhaps a new top every single day. After a long time finally, she asked me to say something about myself.

I just said there was nothing unusual about me. I told her that I also loved chicken, rajma and chaval. Then I added that I had completed my tenth in DAV school. When nothing more came in my head, I said, "You ask me what you want to know, and I will answer."

She asked nothing and left the rest for the future.

◆

The deepest, strangest and the most stirring memories were indelibly marked with corresponding images of Ashima. My fluency at reading her expressions had reached the point where I could look at her from the corner of my eyes and deduce with accuracy what she was thinking in class.

Soon, she had become part of my daily routine. Whatever I thought, whether it was about studying or of sleeping, her smiling face started dancing before my eyes. Whatever I did, first I thought about her and always gave her top preference.

Days passed; each day was more memorable than the previous one. The more we talked, the more we were coming closer to each other. The feeling of love was increasing day by day; I was becoming more possessive about her.

One day, in tuition class, she came in a very short tight top that ended at her waist, just above the jeans. The boys started hooting in groups as she entered the class. I felt very bad. It wasn't a one-off event; it happened almost every other day.

Later in the class, I saw very vulgar things written on the benches about her. That day I thought that I would tell her to take care and started scratching out those words with a pen.

In the coming days, I became more possessive towards her. I did not like it when she talked to anyone else. Though she was in a different school, I never tried to investigate whether she was talking to any boy or not. I wanted to keep her away from those nasty boys who ogled at her.

Day by day, we were coming closer to each other. We talked a lot at night, almost till 1 a.m. daily. At first we'd speak for fifteen minutes when she'd give me a missed call, and then we studied till 11:30 p.m., sometime till midnight. In between I used to either call her for a minute or message her 'I love you'.

One day, I just asked about her past and said with a different curiosity, "Why have people created such a hype about you? I am hearing things about you from the very first day. I even read very vulgar things about you. The strangest part, even Aftab bhaiya said that you had many boyfriends and that you just use everyone."

She was silent for a moment and then replied, "Actually—"

I interrupted, and asked, "What is your full name? Is your last name Ram?"

"No, Ashima only. Why?" she said as she wondered over my question.

"Actually Aftab bhaiya told me that your name is Ashima Ram. I've heard the same from other people too, but you know I never believed in rumours or what people are saying."

"No. My name is Ashima only."

"No surname?"

"No, there is Kapoor. Actually, there was a friend, Ram Sharma, in class nine. We were good friends. People often say he liked me, but I never felt so. To my surprise, one day he proposed to me and I stopped talking to him. He left Bokaro after class twelve. Since then, we are not in contact," she said calmly and clearly. "And after that, people used to stick his name with mine, adding *Ram* as a surname."

"Did you also feel the same for him?" I asked.

"No, never." Her voice was confident and sharp.

"Okay, I don't have to do anything with your past. I just want your loyalty in this relationship because I love you very much and I also promise the same," I said. "And please try to confine yourself. I don't like people saying anything bad about you. Plus your clothes... Try to wear suits if possible."

"Hmm," she whispered. "How much do you care for me?"

"If I don't care for you, then who would? You are my love." I tried to make the situation normal as it had gotten tense.

"You know Aarush, my friend Tulika wants to talk to you."

"Why? I mean, what should I talk to her about? I don't even know her." I almost stammered.

"Anything. About me."

"Okay. But not now. Later... Okay?" I said, changing the topic.

"Janu, you are a Punjabi. So you must know Punjabi. It's a very sweet language. Teach me some Punjabi," I said.

"You called me janu. How sweet does it sound in your voice! Yeah, I am a Punjabi, but I never lived there," she said, but I interrupted.

"Wait, I know some Punjabi. *Mennu tere naal pyar hai*," I said, trying to recall these words from a movie.

"*Waah*, how sweet. You know Punjabi!" she said with surprise and chortled.

"What do I know? Nothing. Only one line that I heard in a movie. You teach me something," I urged in a childish tone, like a ten-year-old boy.

"Aah, I don't know much Punjabi, but one thing I know very well. *Mennu pata chal gaya si ki tennu mere naal pyar hai aur mennu bi*," she said, but not fluently, though it sounded very sweet.

"This is good," I said naughtily after struggling over the meaning of *chal gaya si*.

"Aarush, can I ask you something?" she said.

"Yeah. Sure, and why are you asking for permission? You are my girlfriend," I said.

"Can I give you a kiss?" Her voice sounded softer than usual and came after a silence.

"What?" I was shocked. "No, what are you saying? Do you know? We must live with some restrictions. Is it not too so early?"

Life's most unexpected things come when you least expect it and the same had happened with me. I was just feeling the world's greatest feelings and now it showed another fragrance, but I thought that I was not ready for that.

She became silent.

"Hello," I repeated thrice, but got no response.

"Ashima, my sweetie. I am not angry. If I shouted, then I am so sorry, but it is too early," I lowered my voice and tried to sound convincing.

"But why did you shout at me?" Her voice was low; it seemed that she was on the verge of crying.

"I am sorry," I said

"I love you Aarush," she said softly.

"I love you too." And she cheered up and I felt relaxed.

We talked for a long time as the next day was Sunday and there was a minor fight about who would disconnect the phone. I used to call her after she disconnected the phone to say I love you. After this, she eagerly waited for my second call.

◆

The Durga Puja vacations had started. Ashima told me that she was also going to Delhi during the vacations. I became angry as she was going, which meant no calls again. But what could she do? Nonetheless, I was not ready to understand. The day before she left for Delhi, she messaged me a cartoon giving unstoppable flying kisses, with the words 'lots of kisses' and 'I love you' three times. I just had a glance over it, and kept the mobile aside and slept.

She called after two days, but we couldn't talk much.

"Hello, listen!" Before I could say anything, the phone got disconnected.

I stood there. My mobile vibrated. It was a message.

"Tulika may call you tonight.

I love you."

◆

The streets were silent. So much so that one could easily hear the rustle of trees in the strong breeze in day time, on the barren road. The mess had been closed, as all the workers were Bengalis and they had gone to their home to celebrate Durga Puja, their auspicious festival. All the dhabas and shops were also closed. We were starving. Somehow we had arranged for some bread and jam and managed for two days. That day, I decided that whatever be the reason, I was not going to stay here during Durga Puja the next year.

As expected, that night Tulika called me. It was very strange for me to talk to her. She told me that she wished to see me. I did not understand what to say to her.

She said, "You are very shy, just as Ashima had told me."

"Okay! Are you in Ashima's section in school?" I had no idea what to talk about, so I asked this question.

"No, I am in the commerce section." she said. "I have known her since class six. How charming and elegant she is. When Ashima told me about you, it filled me with joy to see that she is in love with someone who appreciates her worth, who understands her feelings and cares for her before she says anything."

These words filled me with great joy. I was very happy to hear this.

"She told me that you are a very nice guy, shy and cute. Handsome too," she continued. "You know, I have never heard of Siwan."

When I told her that her knowledge in Geography might be a little weak, she was surprised.

"No, not possible, I scored 96 in Social Science in the boards," she said excitedly, as if she had won some gold medal in a Maths Olympiad and I had doubted her talent.

"So, when are we going to meet?" she asked enthusiastically.

"How can I say?" I said.

"Okay, I will ask Ashima, otherwise she will be jealous. I am leaving now as I have to go to my uncle's home. Okay bye, take care. And enjoy Dussehra. Nice talking to you."

"Same to you," I said and she hung up the phone.

She was open-hearted, and seemed funny too. "Good girl," I whispered and went into the seniors' room.

10

Life resumed as usual. November rushed in. Winter was approaching. Winds were chilly and the sun had started setting early in the evenings. We roamed in the city centre till eight, though usually we used to come back to hostel right before the clock struck seven.

Soon, we paid for the organic chemistry tuition too. In the meantime, we were sent to the St. Xavier's fest where I dedicated a lovely song to her. That very night, she called me, earlier than usual.

"Hello."

"You know, Ashima, I dedicated a song to you. *Lafzoon me kah na sakoon*," I said, excited.

"Is it? Aarush, that's so sweet!" she said, though her voice suddenly turned strangely low. I was sure that something was surely annoying her.

"I think something is bothering you... Did I do anything wrong? Did I offend you by dedicating that song? Or, was the song not a good one?"

"No, stupid. Actually, didi is coming home for her winter vacations in two days. didi and I will be staying in the same room. I am worried about how will we talk if she's around me all the time? You know, I can't live even for a day without talking to you, and we won't be able to meet outdoors as well." Her voice grew sadder with every word she uttered.

I too felt miserable at hearing this. It was a big inconvenience. Also, I had to accept that I too couldn't live without talking to her, even for a day.

"Isn't there any other way to talk to you?"

"No. She sleeps in my bedroom, right beside me ..."

"So, we won't be able to talk as long as your sister stays with you in your room?" I perceived sadly.

"We can do one thing, though. We can speak a lot in these two days."

"But... but how? You don't even have a personal phone," I asked. "And you can't surely call from your landline."

"I have saved some money and I have talked to Tulika. She said she will arrange a SIM card and a phone for me. She will be coming tomorrow."

My heart was brimming over with love as I heartily said. "I love you, janu," planting innumerable kisses on the receiver, lasting for almost two minutes. "You are my sweetheart, my janu, everything... I'm really lucky to have you, honey."

"Me too. You are so sweet... In spite of your seniors' tantrums, you never miss talking to me. You know, at first I used to think that Biharis were not really good people and that they wouldn't have respect for anyone as they were very rude. But you have proved me wrong. I often doubt whether you really are a Bihari. I am so lucky to have you," she said.

I listened intently. Her voice sounded sweet and child-like.

"Me too. Ashima, you know it is not the state or country that decides who is bad. It is the person's attitude that might be wrong, whether he is from Bihar or Delhi... it never really matters," I said, adding, "But, Ashima, how will I be able to contact you, if I want to convey any message to you?"

"Don't worry. Tulika will be calling you regularly. Whatever you want to tell me, you just say it to her. I will be calling her daily," she said. "You know, Aarush, I have never seen such a responsible and caring person like you before."

"But, I am not able to give you the happiness that others do. Not even a moment of joy or a moment of my presence. I am really sorry."

"Aarush, don't you dare say such things to me again!" she yelled. "I know the problems you are facing. I can understand that you are doing all that you can do for me."

"Aarush, can we meet outdoors? Just for once?" She asked me something for the first time. I knew how she was feeling.

"Ok ... Where shall we meet then?"

"Actually, there is a party at Hotel Classic on the eve of Christmas. Only for couples and I want to attend that party, as Tulika is going there too. So, can we meet there?" she asked tentatively.

"What? Tulika has a boyfriend?"

"Yes ... A boy from our school. Ayush."

"Ok. So, what's the party about?"

"Dance, songs."

"But I don't even know how to dance," I evinced my problem.

"You don't know how to dance or you don't want to dance in front of others?"

"No no. I mean, I don't dance at all. I really don't know how to dance."

"Aah! Everyone knows how to dance. It's not such a tough job.

In fact, you won't be so bad," she assured me. "Would you like to dance with me on that day?"

"Yeah, sure... I will try." I was still not very comfortable with that idea.

"Don't worry. I will teach you," she assured me, giggling.

"I will try my best," I tried to assure her.

"I know that you have a problem with that and I know you are saying so only to keep me happy. At least, come to the nearby SBI ATM so that I could see you and have a talk. I want to let my friends know how smart my boyfriend looks."

I laughed at her childish words.

We met as per her wish and talked till morning; it was nearly four in the morning when I had to finally end our call, which I really never liked to do. I always wished that her call would last forever.

Next day, in the evening, she called me from a new number. As her sister's arrival approached, our talks grew longer and more desperately passionate. She called as many times as she could in those two days. After every class, evening, night, and morning. On the last day, she suddenly started weeping.

"Hey, what happened? Why are you crying?" I was stunned.

"Aarush, how can I live without talking to you for such a long time?" she moaned.

"First, you stop crying or I'll start weeping too," I said slowly. My tone cracked with grief as my eyes turned wet.

"I am not crying. I know you too are weeping there. You sound sad and low."

"No, pagli! I am not!" I assured her with a lie.

"I love you Aarush, muaah! You know, even I am joining Surender sir's tuition."

"That's fantastic."

We said lots of – in fact, uncountable – 'I love yous', and exchanged unlimited kisses before ending the call. Actually, I didn't want to hang up, but it got self-disconnected as my balance was finished.

The two days passed by like two long hours. As someone has rightly said, while talking to your beloved one, even a whole day seems like ten minutes, but when you sit over a stove even for a second, it seems like hours. The same was the case with me.

I couldn't sleep for those two days, and maybe, she too laid awake in my absence.

The sun set and the night was too long. My heart filled with nostalgia. The deepest feeling of my heart could be felt in the deep silence of the night. The love story had begun from one side and got accrued only in three months. The absence of your loved ones really tests your love a lot.

It was around ten in the morning when Tulika called me. We had a little chat about ourselves before switching over to the issue of Ashima and me.

"You are really sweet and caring. Ashima is really lucky to have you."

"Thanks. You too are very sweet. I don't know you much, but Ashima always speaks about you," I sighed and continued. "She called me only an hour ago and I am already missing her."

"She called me a little while ago too. She was very upset ... just like you are right now."

"Thanks for arranging the SIM and the phone. I really don't know how I can pay you back for this great favour," I expressed my gratitude.

"It's nothing like that. You both are very precious to me. You don't know how happy I am to have you for Ashima." She sounded emotional.

"I had been endlessly talking to her for the last two days – evening, noon, morning and night. And the credit goes to you for all this," I giggled. "By the way, how much did it cost?"

"Aarush, please leave that. You know, Aarush, she was never like she is now. She has changed herself a lot for you. In fact, I never saw her like this before. You know what... never before, she had worn a suit, but after she met you, it was unbelievable to see her that way. I never saw her being serious and caring for anyone before, not even for me. She really loves you so much. And you too rightly snatched my sweet sister," she said. Her last sentence came with a giggle.

I was listening intently.

She continued, "When she told me that you have rejected her proposal, I knew that you are different from the others. I really wanted to meet you."

"Yeah sure, I too want to meet Ashima's lovely friend," I said, excited. "Maybe we can meet in the Chinmaya school fest."

"Yeah, sure. That would be great. I will have to ask Ashima for permission to meet you," she said affably, laughing again. "She told me that you are very possessive about yourself too."

I hummed.

"You know, her birthday is coming. It's on 8th January. You know, every year, I'm the first one to wish her. And, even this time, I will be the first one," she challenged me. I accepted the challenge and we both set our watch with a reminder.

At the end of the conversation, I asked her to let Ashima know that I love her very much. She promised me she would.

11

Days suddenly seemed restless, crawling away slowly. I started cursing the fact that painful days always passed very slowly while joyful days passed in the blink of an eye.

I was becoming impatient as I didn't get a call from her in the next ten days.

Tulika often called me to know about my well-being and conveyed my messages to her. "She too is missing you very badly, but she is in no position to call you. She calls me daily and reminds me to call you," she said. "Even now, Ashima is online on my landline."

One night, she messaged me that the Christmas party she had asked me to attend with her was cancelled. I instantly realized that she was lying to me, and started cursing myself for not fulfilling her wish. "I couldn't do a thing for her. How would it have harmed just to be with her ... just to sit along for a moment?" I was grief-stricken. Tears of anguish flooded my eyes and my heart puffed with the pain of her memories. I was eagerly waiting for her sister to go back.

Next day, I came early to the physics tuition class so that I could see her after a long time, but my wish soon vaporized when she didn't show up even after fifteen minutes. I was strolling on the pavement outside the tuition centre. Students came by, parked their cycles and went to the classroom. Ten more minutes for the class to start, I thought with a sharp look at my watch. "Where is she? Hasn't come yet …" I was strolling, my eyes fixed on my shoes.

Soon, a green coloured scooty zoomed into the lot and halted with a screeching sound. "Didi, slow down." I raised my eyebrows. Ashima stood near the pillar. A girl, a little older than her, was parking the scooty.

I came closer, but not very close, and pretended that I wasn't curious about them. She was of normal height, with a fair complexion like Ashima, but slightly healthier than her. Her long hair was oiled and plaited at the ends. Her face resembled Ashima's, and that confirmed that she was the IITian sister, Aakriti Kapoor. Soon, my eyes filled with appreciation. Today, I didn't even pass a smile out of the fear of getting caught. But, she smiled back graciously. Pavitra too rushed down and joined them. Now and then, I raised my eyes to see her and, to my surprise, I saw them laughing while all the pairs of eyes stared at me. I realized they were talking about me. Soon, I heard a voice.

"*Smart. Isn't he?*"

"Looks like Samir Soni, doesn't he?

"Intelligent too."

"Yes, but don't disturb him."

I stared at them, a little amazed, wondering if what I had heard was true or just a misconception of my ears. I was right. All the pairs of eyes were still staring at me. I turned away and made my way to the class.

"Very shy. Shy like a girl. Maybe even more …"

At night, she messaged me that the girl with her was her sister. She was telling Ashima not to disturb me as I looked studious. A smiley sign accompanied 'I love you' at the end of this message.

The ominous clouds that had gathered over us, slowly drifted away, and soon, the shadow of desertion faded too. Her sister left after ten days; meanwhile, I talked to Tulika thrice to convey my messages.

We joined the organic chemistry classes. The t eacher was boring, slow, and narrative and disciplined; he used to enter promptly at 6:30 p.m. and leave us exactly after an hour and a half. The class used to be very calm, as all the back benchers either slept or got engaged in messaging their girlfriends. Even though he taught us well and his explanations were exceptionally brilliant, he was supremely boring and horribly slow.

Firoz often got irritated and whispered a few abusive phrases, "*Kamina ...*" I giggled at his frustration. I too got irritated, but we had no other choice.

Mayank often bunked classes or came along with his girlfriend, Smiriti, my classmate. She was from Patna.

One day Mayank came over, smiling broadly, and sat beside me, explaining with alacrity that he had kissed her downstairs. Needless to say, I was more than amazed.

"Kudos," Firoz said. His smile was broader this time. "How did you do it?" As I wasn't really interested, we swapped our seats. Firoz shifted into the middle seat while Mayank and I were left at the corners. Despite that, I could hear bits of their conversation.

"You know, no one was on the staircase. I just held her tight without letting her know… around her slender waist. Oh my god! What a waist she has got! So thin, so sexy that I couldn't stop myself. When she turned around, astonished and surprised, I put my lips over those puffy and thin lips and smooched hard," Mayank said coyly and smiled at his achievement.

Firoz was listening with rapt attention. In fact, he had never been so attentive to anything before. "What happened next?" Firoz asked curiously.

"Her eyes widened, but she kissed me too. It felt awesome, her sweet, juicy lips. Aah!"Mayank said touching his own lips.

Firoz looked at Smiriti. Perhaps he was imagining himself in Mayank's position.

They whispered throughout the class, giggling.

◆

As days passed by, Mayank's obsession to have sex with Smiriti grew. They started coming late to classes and sometimes, they entirely bunked the classes.

One day, when they entered, I noticed that Smiriti's top was not in proper place and her bra strap was visible. I understood what might have happened, but I didn't ask Mayank about it. I knew that he himself would soon tell us everything.

The class was going on when my mind was suddenly distracted by the vibrations of a mobile. It was Mayank's. He read his message and smiled meanly.

"So, sweetie, studying?"

He replied, "*No, looking at curves.*"

I was annoyed with the repeated vibrations of the phone and hissed at him to set his phone on silent mode. Without a word, he obeyed me.

Another message was received: "*You dirty boy, no more teasing*."

When Mayank smirked, I raised my eyebrows at Smiriti. She was looking towards Mayank.

Soon, their act grew and they started bunking classes periodically.

◆

Needless to say, one thing led to another and they soon found a way to have desperate sex after exchanging so many furtive kisses and sensual messages.

As decided, they booked a room in a hotel, a little away from the main market, and one Sunday, they both left for that secretly booked spot.

As the two entered the room, Smiriti came nearer to the bed, while Mayank followed her, closing the door behind him. Both were staring into each other's eyes and didn't say a word as strange feelings crept upon them for the first time. Soon, Mayank raised her face, stared at her with rapt attention and slowly brought his lips close to hers. And now, it was only two millimeters away and finally, he rubbed his lips over hers. Mayank didn't move an inch for a few minutes and started sucking her pinkish lips, moving over to her tongue. Initially, she resisted casually, but later, she too started enjoying the pleasure and co-operated. In fact, so passionately that she started to bite his lips.

"Aah! Darling, what are you doing?" Mayank screamed.

"Kissing you."

"Like this? It's wild."

"Mayank, you too kiss me and start feeling it," Smiriti said.

She was licking his lips passionately and was oblivious to his acts... that he was slithering his hand inside her top. Mayank moaned a bit in excitement, when her flaccid breast pressed hard against his chest. In his excitement, he moved his hands higher until he touched her bra, started fiddling with her bra and, suddenly, unhooked it.

She moaned when Mayank moved his hands slowly towards her front and said, "First remove my top," and continued kissing him as he unbuttoned her top. "Please take this off."

Mayank was waiting for this moment and, without lapsing any moment, he removed her top completely. The next moment, he couldn't stop himself from saying, "Wow!"

She stood half naked now. The pink bra was hanging loosely over her breasts. Suddenly, he slipped his hands inside her bra.

"Aah, M-Mayank, what are you doing? Please, don't do this. I am getting out of control," Smiriti moaned in excitement but Mayank chose not to listen to her and continued fondling her breasts.

"Janu, it is so soft and firm too, and perfectly curved. It is so sexy," Mayank hissed near her ears, relentlessly pressing her boobs. Soon, both were out of control as Smiriti too started enjoying the pleasure. Beneath her pleasure, there lay the smell of the innocence of a beginner.

Mayank was kissing, pressing her body, as he caressed her flabby, soft breast with both hands. Mayank was on the pinnacle of excitement.

After about ten minutes, Smiriti turned back, smooched him hard and said slowly, "Who will take off my bra? Please, you do it."

Mayank easily pulled it off, making her breasts bra-free. He stared incessantly at her tempting breasts.

Smiriti said, "Don't just stare. They don't speak." And smiled naughtily. "Please, take off your shirt. I want to kiss you hairy chest."

She moved a little away and he fell on the bed and said, "Wait! Do you have condoms?"

"Yo, baby. At this age, we always live in hope. Who knows when it might come into use?" At first, he was annoyed, but upon her questioning, he smiled lasciviously and opened his hands to show her a packet of condoms.

Smiriti too smiled lustfully as she started undressing herself slowly until her pants fell to the floor. She slowly slipped off her undergarments too and jumped over him. Now, both were entirely naked.

He lay down beside her on the bed and looked at her. They made love for more than twenty minutes with a few crescendo sounds of 'fuck me, fuck me baby', before Mayank said, "Now, I am over." And he sat up panting as she too settled beside him and kissed him on his cheeks, their hands still caressing their bodies.

"Did you enjoy that?" Mayank said, kissing her neck.

"Very much. You are great in bed. Now, I am no more a virgin. Isn't it great that we made love at the age of seventeen?" she smirked.

She was so happy that she smiled again and started kissing every part of his body. Finally, she sat up and started wearing her clothes.

They had a wonderfully sumptuous dinner before they returned to the hostel.

◆

8th January 2007

I didn't study that night. She gave me a missed call at 11:45 p.m. and I called her back.

"Hello ... Sorry janu. I know it's quite late," she said.

"I thought your parents wouldn't have slept yet," I said quietly.

"Actually, we returned only an hour ago from the city centre. I brought a new dress, two tops and a pair of jeans."

"That's good. Birthday dress! But, two tops?" I was amazed.

"Oh, yes. You know janu, the tops were so nice that I couldn't stop myself from buying two. I was in the mood for three, but mummy scolded me," she said excitedly.

"Good ... Which colour?" I too was excited just like her. I wanted to accompany her in every moment.

"One is blue and the other one red, your favourite colour."

"Wow! Good. It's your birthday in a few more minutes and your love hasn't brought any gift for you," I said in a low voice.

"Hey, you do not need to buy me anything. You be with me and talk to me. I don't want anything else. What can any girl in this world wish for more than a boyfriend who loves her more than his own life? I wish that we live together forever. That's my only wish," she asserted.

"I am always with you. And I too want us to live together."

Tears rolled down my cheeks at the very thought of our separation. "You don't know, Ashima, what you have brought for me. You are my happiness, my awaiting love, for whom I was looking for years. How can I let you go? I can't even dare to imagine that, not even in my dreams," I thought becoming slightly sentimental.

"Hold on for two minutes," I said and checked my watch.

It was ten minutes to twelve. Unnoticed by anyone in my room, I closed the door behind me without a noise.

The wind howled and pierced my body. The temperature had dropped to three degrees. I had put on only a half sweater and was in my bermudas. But, I didn't care.

The soft night light was gleaming from the moon that was semi circular, growing brighter with every moment. Its faded light was creeping slowly over the ground, giving twilight's appearance. I looked at my watch, but it was not visible clearly. I moved my face closer to the watch and adjusted it such that moonlight got streamed over it, making it slightly visible. I was excited, but as calm as the moonlight.

It was 11:58 p.m. now. Every minute, every second, seemed important and more enthralling than the India and Pakistan cricket match. My heart was pumping up with the ticking seconds hand in the watch, with an unknown excitement.

I kept looking at the watch constantly and never let my eyes slip off from it. It was a matter of love and friendship and, any how, I had to prove that love always wins.

"Aarush, Tulika is on the landline. I now hold two phones to my ears," she said. "It is really fascinating. It has never happened before."

"Hmm," I whispered. I didn't say much, but listening to this, I too wished that someone should have wished me on my birthday this way; so lovingly, anxiously and happily.

All of us were silent.

11:59 p.m. ten more seconds. I kept my gaze over the watch, drew it closer. Eyes were fixed on the seconds hand.

Thirty seconds ...

Forty seconds ...

Fifty seconds ...

Fifty ninth second ... As the seconds arrow slipped to twelve, words ejected out like they were pre-recorded.

"Happy birthday, happy birthday to you, Ashima my sweetie, my janu," I wished and sang the birthday song as seconds ticked onto twelve. And punched a kiss on the receiver.

She giggled.

"Who won?" I asked excitedly and impatiently.

"What do you mean by 'who won'?"

"Oh, I forgot to tell you. Actually, Tulika and I had challenged each other on who would wish you first."

"Wow! So sweet! You! You wished me first." She was excited.

"*Wooooooo*! I won. Thank god," I was excited. "Love always wins."

"Aarush, Tulika is calling you."

"Okay.,." I said as I too realized that her phone was on wait.

"Hello, I won," I blurted with a wonderful giggle.

"No, I won, she lied," she said, trying to claim the win.

"Ok, why would she lie? Ask her."

"Ok, you won," finally, she gave up. "I am going to her home tomorrow."

"That's nice. By the way, what gift are you giving her?" I asked.

"Don't tell her. I am presenting her a pendant. She had liked it very much when we were once in the city centre. I brought the same for her. And lots of chocolates too; two boxes."

"That's really nice. She will be very happy. She likes chocolates a lot too. Oops ...! I wish I could meet her," I said the last sentence with despair.

A few beeps made me realize that she was on wait. After a short while, I said, "Tulika, can we talk later? Ashima is calling me."

◆

"Aarush, it's my best birthday ever. No one has ever wished me with such alacrity before, as you did now. When someone cares for you, it really feels so good."

I smiled.

"Who else wished you?" I asked.

"My sister, mummy, papa, Pavitra, Divya, and some other school friends too."

"I wish we could share these moments together, looking into each others' eyes for a long time. I wish I could see your face in this romantic moonlight, sparkling and illuminating with shyness, with a lovely saccharine smile that may be the single reason to live the whole life. I want to give you the world's greatest happiness," I said this with a greater ease.

"Wow, Aarush. I never knew that my boyfriend was so romantic. His secret traits are slowly oozing out. Handsome, shy, good natured! And now, romantic too! I am feeling like I'm on the top of the world," she said excitedly.

"Ashima, I really want to share this moment with you, looking into your beautiful eyes, but..." My voice grew weaker.

"Don't worry sweet heart. I am always with you.

12

The annual fest date had been declared as the 21st of January. We were all very excited about this event.

21st January 2007

When I told her about the school fest, at first she protested saying that girls would propose to me, but later, when I told her that I wouldn't go if she wished so, she agreed to let me go.

"Go, but come soon. Wait! Hold on or disconnect the call."

"What happened?"

"Didi is calling me. Disconnect the call. Why do you always ask questions? She is on wait."

I hurriedly disconnected the call, as her hurried tone seemed like Pakistan had suddenly attacked India without a warning.

After five minutes, she called back, sounding much relieved.

"Didi called me. She was asking about the phone being busy. I lied that I was talking to Pavitra. You know what, Tulika is going to come to your school fest. She wants to meet you."

"Yeah, she told me that. But, I wonder how I would recognize her. I mean, I have never seen her before."

"That's quite easy. The fattest girl would be Tulika." And she laughed.

I too laughed at her way of describing her best friend.

On the day of the fest, we all were very excited. Everyone was wearing their best dresses and impressive outfits, including me. Firoz took more than half an hour for his make-up and, time to time, he preened himself in front of the mirror, constantly asking others, “Am I looking handsome enough?”

I had put on cream coloured cargos, which I had bought during Diwali, but I didn’t have a contrasting t-shirt. So, I borrowed a black shirt from Saksham, just as the others too were borrowing shirts from him; he had a nice collection of shirts.

When I was buttoning the shirt, Tulika messaged me.

“Am in the school. In yellow top and brown pants.

Call me when you reach”.

I rushed down and saw that others were ready too, waiting for me.

We hired an auto and reached Chinmaya in ten minutes.

“It seems that we have reached quite early. See, people haven’t come yet. We are left with a plenty of time,” Firoz said, peering out from the side of the auto.

I cheered up looking at the façade of the joyful event that was shaded by a canopy at the entrance gate. I was anxious that Tulika would be waiting for me.

After paying for the entrance tickets, we entered the campus and took a narrow path that was running alongside the outer boundary wall towards the ground, where everything was being organized.

After looking at the hordes of people, I said, “No, we aren’t early. See, so many people have already come.”

“Look, how beautiful she looks! In my language – *maal*!”

Firoz suddenly sprang into action and whistled in his typical tone that he used whenever he saw girls, widening his eyes, indicating Anvesha of section B, the most beautiful girl as per his assumption; in fact, of the whole of Chinmaya.

"Wow! Just look at her. Tight top and fitting jeans. Wow! So sexy, isn't she?" With every word, his eyes grew wider.

I didn't say a thing. For me, Ashima, my love, was the most beautiful and splendid girl on this earth ever.

After a few minutes, I moved towards Firoz who was talking to Anvesha, smiling away to glory. I came over and stood near Firoz and, that was when Anvesha looked at me and turned silent abruptly.

Firoz looked over and introduced me to her, "He is Aarush, my friend from Section C, and she is Anvesha."

"Everyone knows him. He is so handsome; in fact, today he is looking great," Anvesha said, turning towards me, smiling a great deal.

"Thanks." We shook hands. "Thanks for the compliment."

My cheeks blushed and I suddenly felt shy. Firoz looked a little downcast. I bemused on his predicament of jealously. Noticing his jealous looks, I turned towards the gate to leave. Students were flowing into the ground, filling the cavernous space and air with fragrances of different perfumes.

Later, Firoz joined me and we moved towards our seniors who were standing near the game stall, talking to someone. I waited there for a moment when I suddenly remembered Tulika. I looked at the other side of the stalls, searching for a girl in a yellow top.

"Are you looking for someone?" Firoz asked.

"Actually, Shubhashish told me that he would come and message me once he arrives," I lied glibly, discreetly extracting myself from the crowd.

The whole ground was teeming with couples, while those who were single, were looking for girls. Funnily enough, no girl was left single.

Everyone was in their best outfits with attractive make-up. Most of the girls were wearing stylish high heels, which I noticed very carefully were painted diligently to match their nails. Some of them were either in sleeveless or low cut neck dresses, trying to walk along fashionably with plunging necklines. Even boys looked no less fashionable than girls. They too were adding charm to the fest in their stylish jeans and coloured t-shirts. One of the girls, at whom most of the boys were ogling, wore a very low cut dress, staring at which, boys started jeering and catcalling, when she had bent down to the ground to pick up her handkerchief and her low cut dress slid a little more, revealing her cleavage clearly.

I left the place as I eventually started missing my love.

I found many familiar faces, my friends and classmates. Shekhar too was at the party. I could never know the mystery of his disheveled hair, which always stayed straight, pointing towards the sky. It seemed like every morning he touched a high-voltage wire with bare hands and his hair rose up as a token of respect for his taking care of his hair in such a noble way. If Set Wet or any other hair gel company had seen this, they wouldn't have surely invented their product out of the fear of failure of their product.

I couldn't see Tulika anywhere, so I called her up. "Hi. I have reached the spot. Where are you? I am at the entrance of the fair gate, almost two feet away from the chaat stall."

"I am coming."

After waiting for two minutes, I espied three fat cute girls strolling towards me, and turned around.

"Hello, Aarush." A thin and raspy voice reached my ears.

I turned around to find a girl in a yellow top, flecked with black pants, sporting a cute smile on her face.

"Aarush?" she asked in an interrogative tone, raising her eyebrows.

"Yes… and, you must be Tulika, Ashima's best friend, right?"

She stood barely a foot away from me. She nodded and flapped an amiable hand towards me. This time, her smile got wider, and her eyes shrank. Her hair was short and was falling over the nape of her neck; it was indeed shorter than mine.

I shook her hand, aware of the fact that I had already started sweating despite the fact that it was winter. I wiped it quickly, glancing at her with enormous appreciation for all the help.

"Ashima is right. You are really handsome," she said, smiling broadly. "And you are shy too. Look at you," she teased.

Whenever there was a pause in our talk, I raised my head to look over at the other side for any seniors walking our way.

The ground was crowded, and everyone was babbling out loud; sonority of loudspeakers, shouting of winners was adding a different ambience to the festive atmosphere. Just then, the music band began to play a very romantic song 'Tere bin', which was acknowledged by a huge round of applause. I turned around while a small group of boys and girls started jumping and dancing in excitement.

"Missing Ashima?" she asked, looking at my expressionless face.

I nodded. "This is the song I wanted to dedicate to her."

"So sweet …" she said, taking out her phone.

"May be it's her call," I thought.

"Hello, Aunty. Can I speak to Ashima?" she said.

I was stunned to hear this.

"Hello, Aarush is with me. Talk to him." And she handed over the phone to me. She was smiling broadly. I too smiled, took the phone and had a little chat with her.

"Why didn't she come?" I asked.

"Actually, she was ready to come, but aunty never usually allows her to attend such events."

I saw my seniors entering through the entrance gate; the sight of their arrival instantly made me tense.

"I am leaving now, the bhaiyas are coming," I said hurriedly and took a sharp turn at the corner and departed.

I started roaming at random spots, watching the other girls in their best dresses, gold chains and lipsticks, enjoying with their friends or boyfriends, while my memory itched with Ashima's thoughts. My happiness ebbed out soon, realizing her absence. The band had been playing without a pause, shifting from one romantic song to another, which was acknowledged by a burst of applause from the different groups of the crowd. Soon, I felt lonely and sad without her, without her presence. So, I left the fest.

The same evening, when I was turning over the newspaper, around 7 p.m., Ashima called me. I was more than happy and a smile flickered across my face.

"Hello," I said.

"Hi babu! What are you doing? How was the fest?" she said. She too was happy, as I could sense that from her tone. "Did you miss me? I love you."

"Is there anything to say that I wouldn't have missed you? I missed you. I missed you a lot when I saw the others. I love you too. Aah! It was good. I even met your friend, Tulika." I asked, "So, this time you yourself called me?"

"Why? Can't I call you at this time?" Her tone suddenly sounded grave.

"No, I didn't mean that. You can call me at anytime. In fact, I wish to talk to you all day and night. Indeed, seeing your name on the mobile screen – I mean, the coded name – really makes me happy. I think we can talk for some more time, but this time your mummy, *my mother-in-law*, is usually around you. Isn't she there?" I asked teasingly.

"She is downstairs with papa. He is parking the car in the garage. And they will be going to Apna Bazaar now to get some groceries. So, I think I can talk to my babu for a longer time. And don't be serious I am teasing you," She finally dissolved into giggles. "Oye, first tell me what's this coded name?"

I was relieved to hear her giggles and replied, "Actually, I can't save your original name in the mobile so, I saved it as *Naaj*."

"Why Naaj? Is there something special about that?"

"Guess. My babu's name wouldn't be so simple." This time it was my turn to tease. "My babu is so special ... So should be her name."

She muttered for a few seconds, thinking deeply, "Naaj! Naaj!", and finally said, "Aarush, I can't guess. Please just tell me."

"No, I won't tell you so easily. Guess it for yourself."

I was giggling at the puzzled sound of her voice.

"I can't figure it out. Please tell me. Why do you always tease me? You like teasing your babu so much ..."

"Very much. Okay, I will tell you. Just reverse the letters of Naaj," I said cutely.

"J-a-a-n! Jaan," she spelled out the word slowly, trying to make the sweet sense out of it. "Wow, you mean jaan! Wow! How sweet, babu! I really love you."

"Special name for my special girl." I savoured the moment.

"Very special," she said, her voice filled with sweetness. "You know, Tulika called an hour before and started praising you more than ever. She talked for about half an hour and talked only about you. She told me that I was lucky to have you and that you're very innocent and sweet. She was saying that she saw a glint of enormous love in your eyes for me." She seemed excited. "Really, I am so lucky to have you."

"She too is sweet, though a little chubby."

She laughed and then, suddenly blurted out, "Go, what are you doing here? Go study and complete your homework."

"Homework? What happened? Who are you shouting at?" I asked, amazed. That was the first time I had heard her shouting so loudly.

"My brother, gadha! He is snooping in and trying to listen what I am saying," she said, softening her tone.

"Go, do your homework!" she yelled again.

"Whom are you talking to?" I heard the faint sound of her brother.

"To a friend," Ashima said.

"Friend or boyfriend?"

"Will you go now? Otherwise, I will tell mummy that you have been watching WWF," she said threateningly.

"My brother. He is only eight years old, but bigger than a monster. He has already started blackmailing me," she told me, returning to the call.

"Is he still there? Don't be so angry at him. He is just a child," I said.

"Child! He was saying that he would tell mummy that I was talking to my boyfriend. He has left just now."

"Thank god that you have a younger brother, otherwise ..." I laughed. She laughed too.

"Aarush, I think my mummy is coming. I am hanging up," she said, lowering her tone.

"Is it always possible for us to talk like this?"

"So sweet, but I will give you an answer at night with lots of kisses and an 'I love yous'," she chortled. "Okay bye. I love you. Talk to you soon."

"Bye, I love you too, Naaj."

The call went dead after that.

Sometimes, she called me in the evenings when her parents used to go somewhere or down to park the car. She surely called me at least for a couple of minutes whenever she could grab some time.

Also, at times, she used to call me at the crack of dawn, jolting me out of my reverie, saying sweetly, "Oh, sorry honey. Did I wake you up?" And when I replied with a yes, she enjoyed and teased me. She never missed any chance to call me and I never missed any chance to pick up her call.

The passing days made me fall into devastating love. I couldn't do anything except keep thinking and dreaming about her. I waited for her call with the same impatience, talked with the same enthusiasm and restlessness, even after almost a year's relationship. We never had an opportunity to meet and talk about our love. But one day, though a little later than expected, it finally came.

13

January was about to end. Valentine's Day was coming. I didn't know what to do on that special day, so I bought a card and a red rose and sent them to her through Tulika.

"Aarush! How sweet of you! You have sent me such a lovely rose and card. You are so chweet!"

"Sweet rose for a sweet girl. For my love."

We wished a happy valentine's day to each other exactly at twelve in the night, and exchanged countless kisses; some were long, some were short. I was on the roof and, suddenly it started to rain.

"Is it raining there too?" I asked.

"Yeah, isn't that romantic? Just imagine… you and me, alone on the road and rain drizzling down and we get soaked in water. Our clothes get glued to our bodies, exposing other parts," she smiled wickedly. "And we come closer staring into each other's eyes. And then, an abrupt thunderstorm occurs and I would jump onto you. A little later, our lips are an inch away and you put your puffy lips on mine. Our warm breaths would make the ambience more romantic and we would smooch perfectly and passionately for a long time."

I felt too uncomfortable to say anything when she talked that way, though it felt very good to hear and imagine it.

"Very imaginative and filmy," I teased.

"Aarush, I am being so romantic and you..." suddenly she sounded sad.

"Oh, I am teasing you. I hope this will come true one day. It's so romantic and beautiful." My voice too changed this time to float in a romantic wave.

We talked the whole night. At the end, neither of us was really ready to put down the phone. It was so romantic and lovely.

Winter was almost over. Sometimes, mostly in the evening, a cold breeze blew. School classes had been suspended. Maths classes were almost finished. Physics sir hadn't covered the syllabus yet, and today was the last class.

Sir left the class and we stood up to leave, but someone from the staff entered the room.

"Please sit. I have to make an announcement."

We sat down obediently.

"Registration for the 12th batch is going to start from tomorrow. First come, first serve. We have two batches, three days a week. Monday alternate and Tuesday alternate. Timing has been fixed. You can check the details in the office."

Ashima didn't join Ranjeet bhaiya's class. We registered for the Tuesday alternate batch.

The final exams were about to start within a week. We all were engrossed in its preparation and hardly spoke during the class sessions; lesser than ten minutes. Her exams were about to start on the same day as mine. Somehow, the exams finished and holidays had been declared for two weeks. I came back home, though not entirely happy.

I couldn't get a chance to talk to her at home, with mummy hovering around me the whole day. Sometimes I even slipped out of my house at noon to talk to her.

Finally, I returned to Bokaro two days before the end of the holidays. The seniors' board examinations were going on by the time I came back. Two papers were left, after which I would have to rearrange the room.

In the meantime, the school results were announced; my score was just 76% – a drastic drop from 91. Indeed, I had never secured such a low score. I felt low, though every other friend of mine scored lesser than me – the only fact which relieved me slightly. But my major worry was how I would tell my parents about this disastrous result. Somehow, I managed to reveal it to them and, as expected, they scolded me for my inefficiency.

All my seniors left Bokaro for their native places after the exams. I took a sigh of relief, now that I had no fear and tension about their superiority. We had gone to the station to bid them farewell. After that long program of departure, as I was very tired, I tumbled back to the hostel and had a good nap.

It was about eleven when my phone vibrated in the middle of my slumber.

"Hello," I uttered in a drowsy and slow tone, "Sorry, janu, I can't talk to you now. I am too tired for anything now." My eyes were so magnetized that I wasn't even able to keep my eyelids open.

"No, you have to talk. I am calling you in two minutes," she said, without even asking the reason for my fatigue.

I didn't know what happened after that. I slipped back into sleep within seconds and, for the first time, I missed her call.

The next morning I checked the phone; it showed me a hundred missed calls.

"Oh my god! She called me so many times! She must be really angry by now." I grew pensive.

I didn't have an option but to wait till the tuition class to meet and talk to her.

I looked around and finally spotted her in the tuition class; her eyes were red and her face was down. It looked like she had been weeping copiously for a long time, indeed for the whole night. I simply stared at her and without a word or glance, came back to the hostel.

I was feeling bitterly sorry for my last night's carelessness. As I stood brooding over this in my balcony, my attention broke with the vibration of my mobile. It was Ashima.

"You are so mean!" she complained.

"I am sorry, janu. I am very sorry. I was so tired that I slept very badly," I said with a tone of apology.

"I called you a hundred times and you didn't even respond once. You know, I hadn't slept the whole night. You didn't even notice that my eyes were red, did you?" Her tone was aggrieved. And, finally, she broke into tears.

"I swear I am sorry. I will meet you at the Archie's store. Tomorrow." This was the best I could do to cheer her up at the moment.

Listening to this, she stopped sobbing, though her voice was still low and muffled, stuffed with a cold tone, that once again indicated that she had wept for a long time.

"So, tomorrow you will be coming to meet me? So sweet! My brilliant coaching class will be over by eleven in the morning. Reach on time and we shall meet there." Now, her tone was again as sweet as ever.

She smiled and for that smile, I would do anything. She put down the phone, as I relished the fact that less than twenty hours were left to meet her; a hopeful and lovely future beckoned.

31th March 2007

As my seniors left Bokaro, it was debated regarding who would stay with whom? At last, we decided to stay in the same flat, where Firoz was accommodated my room, while Saksham and Manav stayed in the room next to mine.

The next day, I had to rearrange the room. I had to shift the whole book stacks, bed and clothes to Ritesh bhaiya's room. Suddenly, I remembered that I had promised to meet her at eleven – for the first time outside of tuition class. I left all that I had been doing and rushed towards the Archie's store.

My excitement to meet her made me reach there in just a few minutes.

"She hadn't come yet," I thought looking around as I didn't catch a sight of her. I waited patiently, gasping hard.

After ten minutes, I saw her strolling towards me, carrying a red bag on her shoulder. Tulika was with her too. I smiled; she too sparkled with one.

I moved towards her, smiling a great deal. Tulika strolled into the shop, leaving us to ourselves.

I was looking intently at her. It was the first time that I was meeting her at a place apart from the tuition centre. She was ravishingly beautiful, so cute that I didn't want to avert my gaze from her ever. I was watching her face very intently, to catch every nuance of her face. Her eyes accentuated her beauty and her mascara gleamed. The fragrance of perfume lingered into my nostrils.

From her expression, I could see that Ashima felt the same; taking the enveloping silence as our mutual recognition of shared happiness, I wished that this moment would remain forever like this. I looked at her without blinking, looking straight into her eyes, until she stared at me with infinite satisfaction and said, "Don't look at me like this. I'm feeling shy." Her tone was sweet. She averted her gaze. I smiled as I could see her shyness in her cheeks that blushed pink, while her face reddened.

I sensed her hands touching my hands. My fingers curled around them tightly. They felt warm, and soft.

More than ten minutes passed before we uttered a word. We were looking so intently at each other that I wished to grab all these moments; the most precious moments. My face was so close to hers that I could watch her big pupils dilate and shrink, her lips moving. So close to her that I could smell the floral scent with which I would identify her for the rest of my life. She said something, but I wasn't listening. I was looking at her dimpled cheek when a smile escaped her lips.

"Aarush, I am saying something," she chirped loud, near my ear.

"Haan... Yes?"

"I want to show you something. Look at this," she said and uncurled her fingers.

"Don't do this. Let it be curled. It feels good that way."

But she uncurled it already and said excitedly, "Look at this." I saw mehendi on her palm when she untangled my hand. "Hey, what is this? Mehendi? It's awesome!" I said.

"This is what I was about to show you." She opened her palm and said, pointing at the darkest region, "Can you find the first letter of your name on this?"

"It's so beautiful. But why would my name be there?" I asked, looking puzzled.

"Stupid, when a girl puts on mehendi, she writes the first letter of her lover's name on her palm. Now, find your name. If you can find, it is said to be lucky," she said, smiling.

"Oh, so sweet!" I looked at her with intense appreciation and love.

I glanced at her palm. As my eyes dilated, I said, without looking at her, pointing at a curve that was roughly resembling A in the middle of her palm, "Okay, is it this 'A'?"

"Yeah, it is but it is noticeable and anyone can find this. There is one more 'A' which I had hidden within the other design and you have to find that one," she said. A lovely smile escaped her lips.

"But you asked me to find one, and I found this. Now, you're asking for another one. This is cheating ," I teased.

"Aarush?"

"Okay okay. I am searching."

The design was more complicated than a jigsaw puzzle, more tangled than the path of Bhool Bhulaiya in Lucknow. At least, in Bhool Bhulaiya, if someone didn't find the way to come out, there was a common way that led the person out of it, but this puzzle had neither an entrance line, nor any exit.

I pulled the palm closer to my eyes so that I could get a clearer view as I concentrated on its design.

"If I ever had studied with such concentration, at least I would surely have scored more than 30% marks in the recently held exam of the physics tuition," I thought.

I looked at the tangled design for more than ten minutes but I couldn't found any 'A'. Meanwhile, I sensed that she was smiling naughtily. When I looked up, she stopped smiling, though I could still see a fleck of a smile on her face. I too smiled and looked back down.

"I lost," I said and nodded in a disappointment.

"Stupid, gande, here is 'A', she said, dragging my finger to the side bottom of her palm. A tiny square contained a minuscule "A".

"Oh, here is the culprit," I said with a sigh of relief.

"You know, it was bright red. But, now it has faded. When a lover loves his girlfriend very much, it is said that mehendi ends up really red and mine was really dark. When Tulika and Pavitra saw this, they too said the same thing." Her voice exuded excitement.

My face always beamed whenever I saw her smiling that way. I just wished that her cute smile would envelop her face and her lips forever.

"Ashima, I love you," I said.

She felt shy and lowered her eyes. Her cheeks blushed red with shyness.

"Say it to me."

"No, Aarush, I am feeling shy. I can't..." she said, still looking down and thrusting her palm on her face.

"I love you too," she said but her eyes were still lowered.

"Ashima, it's getting late. Shall we go now?" Tulika asked.

Ashima looked at me. I whispered, "So early! I don't want to let you go. I hope this moment stays on forever."

She nodded, though a moment later, she said, "Aarush, I think I should go. The class ended at eleven and it's almost twelve. Mummy will start worrying now. I will call you when I reach home."

I consented, though unwillingly.

"Bye," said Tulika.

"Bye," I muttered.

Both the girls left, leaving me standing there, seeing them vanish around the next turn. For once, she turned back towards me and smiled sweetly. I smiled too.

Summer was at its peak. A hot breeze was blowing throughout the day, warming the wall, bed and everything; even the fan was gushing out hot air. Firoz and I started studying, sitting up on the roof. Though I had a book opened in front of me, I was actually pondering over how I would talk to her. I decided to go down into the room to study.

"Firoz, I am going back to the room. I am feeling sleepy," I said to Firoz.

"Okay, I will come after about an hour."

I came down and locked the room from inside. It was about quarter past ten in the evening. I was impatiently waiting for her call. She called me at last.

When Firoz came down after midnight, I was lying on the bed, snuggled in a bedsheet. I had no other choice. And, in a few seconds, I was drenched in sweat. It was so hot under the bedsheet that I was starting to feel like a chicken put into a tandoor.

"Hello," I was whispering. Words were barely coming out. It sounded more like I was hissing.

"Where are you? I am not able to hear you properly. You are suddenly sounding so low."

"I came back to the room. I am under the bedsheet," I whispered.

"Why are you under a bedsheet? It's so hot!" she asked; her tone was a mixture of amusement and anger.

"Firoz is in the room. And I have no other choice. And I just want to talk to you. But, you don't worry; we can continue our chat this way. It's only a matter of an hour."

"But Aarush, it is so hot! How will you stay like that for so long?"

"Ashima, I can do anything to talk to you, trust me," I said.

"But…" She was not ready to agree.

"Now, talk to me."

"Aarush, didi is calling me now. Her phone is on wait. Just hold on for a second."

"Now? It's almost twelve! Why does she call at this time?" I said. Irritation edged my tone. "And she called you only an hour ago. Now, she's calling again!"

Before she could listen to my complaints, she shifted my call on to hold. A ray of suspicion started to envelope me. Anyhow, I kept this suspicion out of my mind. My condition was becoming worse. I was almost drenched in sweat; it seemed like I had just taken a bath. It was horribly suffocating, so I pushed my nose out of the bedsheet to manage a breath. I squinted at Firoz; he was looking at me suspiciously, trying to figure out what I was doing. I pulled over the sheet again.

Two minutes later, she called me again. "Did she say anything important to you? She called you at such an odd time!" I asked.

"What do you mean by that? She always calls me at this time. You have any problem with that?"

She construed my tone in a wrong way and I said, assuring her, "No, I didn't mean that. I was just worried that, as she had been finding your phone busy each time she calls you, she might start suspecting you and may ask you whom are you talking to so late at night. That's what I meant."

We talked for an hour more and I had turned literally into a scorching corpse. I went straight to the roof after ending the call and started gulping copious amounts of fresh air.

I talked to her that way for ten days before her acts made me sad, when she refused to talk to me on a very hot night, saying with an excuse, "I can't talk to you now. I am going to sleep in AC in mummy's room."

I tried to persuade her to talk at least for two minutes, but she completely refused. Before this feeling of pain could vanish, a sudden inferiority complex started engulfing me. It wasn't the first time; this feeling aroused from the day when I saw her in a car. Sometimes, she talked a lot, though not intentionally, about herself, her house and her comforts. The same feelings aroused within me when she said that she would be going to Singapore.

"She lives in AC. She has a car. What do you have, Aarush? Remember how you used to sleep in the hot summers in Siwan, without even electricity, leave aside an air conditioner!" A feeling of inferiority started paralyzing me day after day and made me think that I was not up to her standards.

◆

Meanwhile, my father had decided to visit me. He arrived the next day. I received him at the station and showed him around Bokaro.

As he had to leave early the next day, he slept early. I peered over at his bed to check if he was indeed sleeping. I silently crawled out of the room, and dialled her number. Her phone was busy; it remained busy even after trying twice. Busy and busy. Whenever her phone prompted a busy tone at night, my heart took a flight of suspicion, and a series of questions started circulating. To whom was she talking to so late at night? It might be her sister? No, might be her other friend... or some boy. My heart would race until she picked up the phone and revealed whom she was really talking to.

"Hello, your phone says you are busy with some call. Whom you are talking to?" I asked, as she picked it up after my fifth try.

"I am talking to my sister. What happened?" Her voice always appeased me and I always trusted her.

"You know that my papa is here and you still want to talk to me. I know you love me very much."

Next day, in the evening, papa left for Siwan. I accompanied him to the bus stand.

Fortunately, she called me while I was on my way back to the hostel. I decided not to tell her what I had been thinking for the past few weeks.

"Hello, Aarush, where are you? Has your papa left?" she asked.

"Yeah. Just now. I am coming back to the hostel. Ashima, I have to tell something to you," I said slowly.

"What?"

I was silent.

"What happened? What is it that you want to say?"

"How should I start it? I think I am not up to your standards, your status."

"W-what? What are you talking about? I didn't get you." Her voice was a mixture of amusement, confusion and suspicion.

"Actually, I don't know why I get this feeling. You have everything and I don't have anything. I'm a middle class guy, a little lower than that too, if I can say. I am not financially as strong as you are. So, I keep feeling like I am not up to your standards."

"Aarush, have you gone mad? I don't know what made you think so. Have I ever said that I'm a wealthy girl? I too eat and wear what you do. I'm no different from you. I am not some Birla or Tata." I realized her tone was full of seriousness.

A silence prevailed for more than five minutes. And her voice broke the silence.

"Aarush, promise me, you won't say such things again. I know, you have seen me in a car. Maybe, that's why you started thinking this way. My father is in a higher post and so the company has provided him with a car. In fact, everyone has got a car around here. And from now on, we will never be talking about this topic."

I nodded and whispered, "Yeah." At that moment, it felt fine to me.

Meanwhile, a change had come over. Since the day I had told everything to her, most of the times, she called me but we hardly spoke for even fifteen minutes. I started observing another aspect; she started uttering less 'I love yous' than I did, but things weren't the same as before. I was very upset; I couldn't bear to see her like this.

Her silence made me worry more. I didn't say anything further about that conversation, just as she had asked me to. The same behaviour continued for the next few days and weeks. It was painful. But, I didn't wish to lose her. Later, I realized that I shouldn't have discussed all those things with her. I didn't wish to see her face floating down with disappointment.

14

5th May 2007

The next day, when I woke up, it was really late. So, I rushed to the bathroom, my eyes were bleary red. All the others had already left. I pedaled my cycle as fast as I could.

"Hey, stop! Stop!" Someone shouted as I moved ahead. I turned back and saw Shekhar running towards me with the same rumpled hair and a loaded bag on his shoulders. I never understood what he carried in his bag; my bag was so light, only a notebook and a novel.

"Hi, can you drop me to the school on your cycle?" he asked softly.

"Yes, but you have to ride yourself," I said and shifted a on the sitting rod.

"Thanks," he whispered, settling on the driver's seat.

"Good, you are pedalling fast. Hope we can reach before the morning assembly and attendance starts," I said.

When we reached, the assembly had already started. Anyhow, I parked the cycle.

"Hello, boys, park your cycle properly!" the watchman bellowed, rushing forward, when he saw that I had parked my cycle carelessly.

"Who cares?" Shekhar said and he ran. I too followed him.

The prayer was going on. Principal madam wasn't there. Narmendra sir signaled to us to stand aside at the corner of a pillar near the entrance gate. I squinted towards Shekhar; he nodded calmly.

All the students departed to their respective classrooms, except the five late comers, that included me.

Narmendra approached us and asked, "Why are you late?"

We didn't know whom he was asking. He had a side glance, looking from the corner of his eyes.

I shrugged. "Sir..." I said as I thought he was asking me.

"Sir, actually..." Shekhar said. Everything happened simultaneously. I almost laughed. Shekhar too.

"Shut up. Stop laughing. You both, stupid," he groaned. "Reply to what has been asked."

"You start first." I whispered to Shekhar. On the other side, Banarjee sir was dealing with three other boys. "Why is it always the Chemistry faculty who deals with the late comers? They don't have any other work to do or what?" I thought as a smile crawled on my face.

"What happened? Why are you smiling?"

"Sir, it's the Chinmaya logo – 'Keep smiling'," I said in a low tone.

"Shut up! Just shut up. Is some kind of joke going on here?" he said gruffly. His face flowed with anger this time and blood rushed through his temples. I turned serious at this comment and nudged Shekhar with my elbow as he did not even start to say any excuse.

"Sir, actually he gave me a lift. We were on right time, but..." he paused and took a side glance towards me. I gave a suspicious look. Even I didn't know what he was about to say. He paused a bit longer and then continued, "Sir, when we were near the PN colony, a boy met with an accident. So, we stopped to help him." And he bent his head down.

I was listening intently, but after this, my eyes dilated with amazement and shock. I looked towards him, but he was still looking at sir.

"Our humanity didn't allow us to leave him alone," he said.

"What? Humanity? Accident?" Listening this, my eyes became dilated more with shock, surprise and praise for his beautifully scripted lie and imagination. Sir looked at me. I nodded to support this. He felt relaxed and his stretched muscle now looked relaxed. He thought for a while.

"Ok, but don't repeat this in future. This is my last warning," he said in a soft tone. I had never heard his tone so soft. "Go back to your class." We turned back and strolled towards the staircase. I was smiling.

"Already twenty minutes late," I whispered.

Neelanjan sir, aka Golu, was teaching. The whole class started laughing as we entered the room, not at me, but at Shekhar. He was late, as usual; nothing new. I sat beside Shubhashish.

"Summer holidays are about to start. So, I must say, or it's my request for you, to learn C language which I read last year because C++ is similar to C and you can't learn that without knowing C properly," he started softly. But he had no other choice except to shout, as no one was paying any attention. Some were in deep discussion about the last match; some were engrossed in what they had brought in their tiffin boxes. When he finally shouted for silence, everyone went silent. The bell rang and the class ended.

And, all over again, we resumed our work.

"It's chemistry next", Tanmay shouted, "Sir is absent."

Nobody paid any attention, as whoever might come, no one would ever study or pay attention to what was being taught. He made an ugly face and sat down.

A new face entered the room. "Banarjee sir is busy. So, I am a substitute for this period," he said in a plain tone.

"He may be a faculty of some lower class," Tanmay said in a whisper, turning towards a girl, though her intensity was high enough to be heard by the back benchers. I thought the same too, as we all knew the faces of the higher class teachers well. I didn't pay attention and continued my discussion with Shubhashish.

"Mobile checking is going on. Whoever is carrying a mobile, just hide it. Otherwise they will be seized!" A thin boy, whom I had never seen before, shouted.

"Who told you that?" Tanmay asked. It seemed that he knew him. Soon, everyone, who was till then busy chatting and discussing, sat up in rapt attention, especially the hostlers.

"A group of teachers had come to my class; they confiscated two mobile phones. Now, they are in section B," he said and fled. Section B was only adjacent to our class.

"Keeping the phone in the bag would be safe," I thought, placing my phone between the pages of a copy. But I wasn't satisfied. So, I took it out again and hurriedly slipped it into my pocket. Fear could be easily seen on my face.

Sir approached our row and said in a deep tone, louder than usual, "All of you there, empty your bags and show me everything you have."

Shubhashish turned his bag inside out. Books and FIIT JEE package rolled down. I was looking at him.

"Empty your pockets," he said, spotting something visible, protuberating from his jeans.

"Nothing sir, only a handkerchief and nothing else." A hissing sound from the throats uttered.

He fixed his gaze upon me and checked my pocket.

"What is this? A handkerchief?" His sound turned harsh.

I shivered as my face turned dry. Even my moist lips were dry. "Sir, sorry. I will never carry it to school again. I will leave it at home before coming to school." My voice came out in a hiss and I could manage to say only this. My voice was tinged with despair.

He didn't listen to what I said; turned back sternly and moved away. I followed, repeatedly uttering, "Sorry sir, sorry sir."

"Meet the vice principal in his office and collect your phone from there."

My voice faded into melancholy. I sadly returned to my seat.

In the break, I went to the vice principal's office. After numerous arguments and reasons that there would be a chance of it getting stolen from my hostel, he was finally ready to return my phone. They asked me to take it after the class.

I took my phone after the school hour, relieved at getting it back.

◆

That evening, physics tuition was suspended. Ashima hadn't yet reached till then. So I decided to stroll around. After a few minutes, when I was returning, I saw the three of them in front of the building.

"Aarush, have you gotten back your phone?" Ritika asked, as I approached them. It was Ritika Dey, my classmate.

I halted and thought, undecided whether to respond to her or not, as Ashima was nearby too. I nodded and said with an agreeable look, "Yes". I strolled a little closer towards them. I took a side glance and looked over at Ashima; she was smiling with her gaze fixed upon me.

"Okay, that's good," Ritika said, as I averted my gaze from her and fixed it on Ashima. I nodded.

"This is Anita, by the way. I think you know her," she continued and introduced Anita to me.

"This is Ashima, my good friend," she said, giving the faintest whisper of a naughty smile to me. I too smiled, as Ashima flapped her hand towards me to shake it. We shook hands.

"How would he not know me?" Ashima said, smiling broadly amid her shining teeth. At one corner, two teeth overlapped upon each other.

I drew myself a little closer to her. Ritika and Anita strolled away from us, laughing endlessly. Ashima was still on the scooty, wearing a yellow top, flecked with some black spots, adding extra beauty to her top and to her. Nearly after one month, I was looking at her so closely. I was happy, certainly I happier than I had been in a long time.

"You are really rocking; a long red kurta and a cream coloured, striped pant. A good combination," she said. Upon seeing us both, Anita and Ritika sauntered away towards the other side of the road.

I nodded.

"You too are looking good. The new top really suits you best," I said, coming closer to her scooty, nearer to the rear view mirror.

I was set aflame by Ashima's nearness, by her bare arm moist against mine, and by the perfume she had put on. I was floating over the waves of happiness. Now I understood why she always wanted to meet and spend some time with me.

"No, it's didi's top. I liked it and she gave it to me," she said. She bent a little lower; her top fell loose at her neck. Seeing her in that way convulsed me with a different sensation. "Aarush?"

"Yeah?" I said, astonished by the way she called my name.

"Give me your hand. I just want to hold it. It has been a month since I held your hand." She twisted her face and said, resting it on my forearm. I too wished to hold her hand, though I couldn't say that to her right then because of my shyness.

I placed my hand in hers, tenderly.

I could feel the warmth of her hand, its tenderness. A wave of excitement swirled in my body. I too squeezed her hand, as she gave a satisfied smile.

"Tuition is finished. What are you all doing here, now?" I asked.

"Actually, Ritika's tuition is up there. Her maths tuition is at six in the evening. So, I drop her every day and then leave for home," she said, pressing and rubbing my hand. I came closer to her; my nose filled with her soft fragrance.

"But, it is only half an hour past four. That means, you can stay here for an hour more." I said, glancing at my watch.

"No, I will leave only after I'm done talking with you and hope this talk would continue forever," she said and smiled.

"Very funny," I laughed and made an ugly face to tease her, pushing out my tongue.

"Aarush, you mean boy," she said and nudged me with her elbow.

"Where have they both gone?" I asked looking around, but there was no sign of them.

"They know about us. So they left us alone to let us talk. Aarush, forget about them. Concentrate on me. Your girlfriend is in front of you and you are worrying about others. You are very bad," she said.

"I love you. I love you very much." I turned around and said, looking directly into her sweet, delectable eyes.

She felt shy. And she bent her head again. Her cheeks blushed with red and pink, which made her look sweeter and cuter. I wished that I could capture this moment in my camera and put my camera running in a repeat mode.

"Aarush, didi is coming in ten days. Her college holidays start from today, but due to some course, she decided to come after five days. And I don't know after how many days she will leave. Maybe, she'll stay here for two or three months," she said.

Beneath all the jollity, tenderness and solitude, I sensed the disturbing tension within us and in her voice.

"We will talk about this later," I said to relieve ourselves from this tension for a while. Meanwhile, I sensed a wave of tension arousing within me, but I didn't want to spoil this moment; an unforgettable moment.

She chuckled, and I did as well.

"Give me a kiss," she said, smiling broadly. She leaned towards me and I could sense the teasing in her tone.

"*Kis*s? Are you mad? Here? Now?" My eyes popped out in astonishment.

"Yeah, at least, on my cheek," she chuckled.

"You are out of your mind. If you insist more, I will have to go, I tell you," I warned, trying to sound harsh, forcing myself to put some anger in my tone. But, the next moment, I realized it was of no use. I was unable to be angry at her.

She was smiling incessantly. "See, there's no one around here, not even a single bird. Even the staff are in the cabin, shops are all closed. Now, you have no excuse."

She was right. Due to the intense heat and high temperature, nearly all the shops were shuttered down and no one was lingering on the road.

"Now, you shut up. I am going," I said sternly and moved away slowly, a mere acting.

"Aarush, stop!" she got down from her scooty and held my hand to stop me. I stood rooted to the spot. She rushed forward, looked around for a moment and, even as I heard an approaching gasp, she smacked a kiss on my cheek, right when I was about to turn around to leave.

My eyes dilated to see her boldness. When I was about to stare at her, her lips momentarily got locked with mine. A romantic whim, a feel, touch of her smooth, fluffy lips. I was floating on the absolute wave of desire and excitement. I pinched myself to confirm it was all real. There was something so enthralling, benign, and sweetening about the past moment. There was something childish in her awesome kiss.

I looked around to check again. There wasn't anyone around. I was relieved and gave an astonished look.

She halted and a childish, cheerful and naughty giggle escaped her lips.

I saw that Anita and Ritika were coming back. I tumbled back, putting some distance between us, and frowned at Ashima to indicate that someone was approaching.

She too turned and looked. With a silent bye, I left that place.

I returned to the flat, relishing the thought of the kiss – a lovely, sweet, moreover, an unexpected kiss. I couldn't have been happier. That was, until there came a sequence of events which eclipsed my love.

15

It was nearly 10:15 p.m. when I went up to the roof. I put the bulb in the holder, and fixed the table in alcove, placed the chair, and started studying, 'Work power and energy' – the same topic which sir had taught in the morning class. I tried to solve the problem and constantly kept glancing at my phone. Sometimes I pressed a button to ensure if there was any missed call or not, as I might have missed it or didn't sense the vibration. But there were no missed calls. I turned the notes, turning pages, taking side glances on mobile. My mind was on the mobile rather than on the notes.

Time passed and it was almost 10:40 p.m.

After five minutes, she gave a missed call. I called her back.

"Why are you so late?" I almost yelled at her. "I have been waiting for almost twenty minutes."

I lowered my voice. Her delay in calling had made me impatient.

"Actually, papa took away the phone with him. Generally, he keeps the phone on the table after coming from office," she said.

"You know it very well how impatient I am for your call," I screamed at her with ferocity. My face blushed red with anger.

"Don't be angry. I was also waiting for the phone. In fact, no one has slept yet." Her voice sounded plaintive, childish, and soft.

And the phone got disconnected. My anger roused again. I dialled back. It started ringing, ringing, and ringing. Again I dialled. It rang for a long time. No reply.

"Where did she go, so early?" I thought. I must have called some ten times. No reply. I got frustrated by such behaviour and called again.

"Hello." A harsh and deep voice groaned on the other side.

"Hello," I said in a creepy and slow tone. Hearing some other voice, I thought it was a wrong connection and disconnected the phone.

"Who was that?" My heart pumped out, beating wildly.

"Was it her mother?" I thought, dismayed and amazed.

I called again.

"Hello!" Again the same voice said gruffly, little louder than before. A lump of fear pumped inside me and sweats appeared on my face. My anger soon faded away.

I disconnected the phone without delaying any second.

My mind was wandering from here to there. "Was she her mother on that side? But how she would pick up the phone?" Thinking this, my heart gave a palpitation and I became afraid of thinking of the future, a future without her, without her phone, without her chatting, no waiting in the night, those sweet talk, infinite kisses each night, those silly questions, giggling, and teasing. I shivered thinking this. The lump rose higher choking my throat. Fifteen minutes passed. I switched off the light.

Twenty minutes passed. A wave of tension got swirled across my body. "What to do?" I thought while strolling. I called Tulika but her cell was switched off.

I thought, walking on the roof, and kept my phone in my hand.

Different thoughts were coming to me, and each time, I

shivered to think what would happen. I came near a gap in the roof and kept my head down.

A little later, my phone vibrated.

Her land line number.

I became frigid, astounded and bewildered, seeing that number.

"Her mother must be calling, as generally the landline is not kept in her room, especially at night," I thought. "What was the need to call her so many times?" I started cursing myself. I didn't pick up. Again, call. Full ring vibration. Again, I didn't pick up. A message came. It read:

"Mummy came and caught the phone. Pick up the phone. Ashima here."

As I finished reading, phone started vibrating. I hurriedly picked up the phone.

"Hello," I said in a feeble tone. "What happened?"

"Mummy came. You were calling continuously and she caught the phone. She took the phone away with her," she said slowly. "I don't know what will happen now. She was very angry at me. Maybe, no more phone from tonight."

"Hello, listen!" I shouted but the phone went dead. The drowsiness of silence prevailed. The helplessness I felt was like a fish without any water around it. I shrunk in gloom. I didn't know for how much time I walked on the roof and came down, thinking about the future.

Next day, in the evening, we had our physics tuition.

"Oh, it's 4:15 p.m. I am late," I grinned when I saw the mobile; time flickered on the top of the screen. I rushed to my room and put on my trousers. T- shirt was the same and I ran for the tuition class.

"Sir has gone to class," one of the staff said.

I rushed to the classroom. I opened the gate with a jerk as usual. My eyes searched for Ashima. She sat there between Ritika and Anita, on the third bench. She also looked at me; the whole class looked at me. I silently looked for a space to sit, but I couldn't find any seat, so I moved to a chair. I hated to sit on a chair, but today I had no other choice. I dragged a chair and sat there.

I was not able to pay attention, so I pretended to write. After every five minutes, I glanced over at. Sometimes sir also saw me, and pointed at me to write, but didn't say anything; he knew I was a sincere student.

I was eagerly waiting for the class to get over. I didn't write a single line. I sat with my head down, thinking about what had happened that night, and of its consequences.

After coming out from the class, I looked around. No sign of her. I looked at her scooty; it was still there. I became angry, and thought, "I am tensed; I don't know where she is roaming. Doesn't she care about us and our relationship?" And I moved ahead to look for her.

She was with Divya, chatting with her, maybe waiting for me. I thought and strolled towards her. She saw me and said something to Divya. After this Divya moved aside, and stood at some distance.

"I was looking for you," I almost panted. Before she could say anything, I said, "What happened at night?" This time my face became strained.

"Mummy came, and she caught the phone," she said. Her voice grew slower. "Maybe from now, it won't be possible to talk at night."

"Why? How will we talk now? You know it very well," I almost cried.

"How would I know? It was not my fault," she shouted for the first time.

I remained silent, gazed at her, astounded and puzzled.

"Aarush, you tell me what should I do? I am also worried. Even I tried to hide the phone but unfortunately you called so many times. Mom became suspicious and took the phone away with her. What could I do? You don't know what my mom has started thinking about me. She thinks I don't study at night," she said lowering her tone, an exasperated tone.

I remained silent, but I was impatient. I wanted everything to be normal like before.

"Now, how will we talk?" I repeated this question.

"It's not possible to call you from home, especially at night. I know mom is not going to give me the mobile. Maybe she will check every night whether I have the phone or not?" Anxiety edged her tone. "I will call you from the PCO, that one rupee coin phone, after the school gets over."

"But it will last only for five to six minutes. Moreover, how much you will spend on this?" I asked.

"We don't have any other choice. In addition, we will meet after tuition and talk. It would be romantic, and lovely, to talk with you, walking with you, and holding hands," she said sweetly and firmly.

I nodded. "What can I say?"

Then, Ritika came. "Ashima, we should go now, it is too late," she said to her, without looking at me. Ashima looked at me with serene and tranquil eyes, lit with hope and consolation.

I squirmed with discomfort. I gasped and looked at her.

"Bye....oh! I forgot to give you one thing," she said. Ritika came back with her scooty, a tangerine one, while Ashima was busy taking out a pink coloured lockable diary.

"This is my personal diary in which I wrote everything about us. Please keep it safe. I know mummy is a little suspicious. So, It's not a good idea to keep it at home," she said and handed it to me.

Then she left the place with Ritika. I stood there, watching her till she disappeared. She once turned to say bye.

At night, I waited for her call. Even when I knew she was not going to all. After every five minutes, I looked at my mobile screen. I didn't realize when I slept.

This was the first night after a long time when we hadn't talk. I also checked in the morning. No pending notification, only a wallpaper of lord Krishna, laughing, may be laughing at me, at my loneliness, at my pain. Perhaps enjoying my pain.

Today was the last class before the summer holidays in school. All the students were enjoying and were planning the holidays.

I was looking somewhere else, outside the window, drowned in thoughts unaware of what was going inside the class. When I realized the class had finished, I came back to the hostel in twenty minutes, drenched in sweat, hot and frazzled. And I slept.

As usual, tuition was suspended in the evening. Without arguing with the staff, I started rambling. My phone vibrated. It was a message.

"*Wait for me near tuition. Am coming. ILY*"

To pass time, I went inside a gift shop. After coming out, I caught the sight of Ashima. She stood at the corner of the arcade, looking around, searching for me. Ritika was at some distance away from her. I thought of teasing her.

I rushed to her. Ritika saw me. I indicated by keeping a finger on mouth, not to shout. She smiled.

"Huhhhh!" I scared her.

She jumped and started screaming and turned around. I laughed out loud.

She was wearing a light blue short shirt, and a black pant. I saw her for the first time in this outfit. She was looking like a sweet well-dressed air hostess.

"You cheapo, you love scaring me!" she said, sounding very childish, and slapping me on the hand.

I laughed, seeing her fearful face, and said, "I love to tease you and love you because I love my love a lot."

Ritika was also smiling.

Ashima stood near the pillar. I came closer to her. "Where have you been? I came five minutes back," she said. Her fearful face was looking beautiful, but not more than when she smiled.

"I was in Retolias," I said. "But how did you manage to come here? And how did you come to know about the suspension of tuition?"

"Simple. I told mom that I am going to a friend's home for class notes and I came here to meet you, to meet my janu, my love," she said.

"So sweet. You know, last night I missed you very much. A night without your call, and our lovely conversation. I missed you very much," I said and faded into melancholy.

"I missed you too. See, this is what I have written," she chuckled, forwarding a piece of paper. "Read and tear it."

It was a long letter, written on both sides. I kept it safely in the pocket.

"Janu, when are we going to talk again at night?" I asked.

"I don't know. But we will meet like this after tuition. You don't know how badly I missed this. You know when I see others talking to their boyfriends, I felt jealous that I have such a handsome boyfriend, but I am not lucky enough to see him and meet him," she said in a gloomy tone, a tear rolled down her cheeks.

"Why you are sad? It is not always necessary for lovers to stay together, to walk hand in hand; it is the love we feel in his or her absence," I said, wiping her tears. "Don't cry, be my girl, my love. You always look sweet and cute when you laugh." I stretched her cheeks and she broke into giggles.

"I love you, I really love you. You are really a very nice person and I'm proud to have you," she said. This time she became emotional. Me too, and was on the verge of crying but I controlled myself. Someone has said correctly that you can't hide true love, your eyes speak of your love for anyone. After so much effort, I couldn't stop my tears. But I giggled.

"Ashima, we must go now. We said that we are coming in fifteen minutes, but it has been more than half an hour," Ritika said, coming closer to us. I drew myself apart from her.

"How half an hour has passed! It seemed that I came just minutes earlier," Ashima whispered. "Now, I have to go. We will meet tomorrow." She looked at me. It seemed her eyes were asking for consent from me.

I remained silent, looking at her face. She knew I wouldn't say anything so she turned back as Ritika was starting the scooty.

I unwillingly let her go. "I love you too." And a tear rolled down my eyes. This time I couldn't keep it under control. And I turned back to go my own way.

"Aarush, Aarush," she shouted but I didn't turn back. I knew if I would turn back, I would start crying. Maybe she also knew this so she didn't call out again.

16

I went up to the roof. No one was there. I took out the paper and unfolded it. It was a big page, written on both sides with a diligent handwriting, though the letters were bigger than mine. Everything by her was important to me. My cheeks blushed and I started reading:

Dear Janu,

I know you are missing me very much. Me too. But what can I do? Nothing is in my hands. I will call you after school. Maybe for ten minutes, but surely I will call you. I also can't live without you. I pray that these bad days end soon, and we talk again like before, small jokes, some pjs – those lovely conversations.

My darling, I have never thought about a person like you, who will be my boyfriend... who is responsible, handsome. You don't know you look like Samir Soni – super handsome and studious. What should I say... you have all the qualities of a perfect person. But you have a small flaw, you get angry easily. Don't worry. I will never do anything wrong so that you never get angry. Otherwise, I will smack a kiss on your lips and lock it so that you can't say anything. I know my kiss will cool you down. You sonu babu.

My life, you are a morning for me and a evening setting sun. Perhaps, you don't know that how long I have waited to walk with you, to talk to you looking into your eyes; walking hand in hand is always a great pleasure. Now, I am happy that we could have all this.

I have been blessed many times. First, you dared to fulfil my dream; you walked with me. You talked to me every night despite all those troubles. I even wanted to talk to you when your father arrived in April.

My darling, there is so much more that I want to say, but the bell has rang, not allowing me to continue this. I love you, I love you. Now I am ending this. I know you will reread this thrice before tearing it up. Tear it after reading.

Your loving girlfriend,

Ashima Kapoor
With lots of kisses.

As predicted, I read it thrice. I was touched. My heart filled with more love for her. "She thinks a lot about me," I thought. "Why do I get angry with her? But what could I do? I don't want to live alone without her, without her calls. I love her so much, the only girl I wish to love my whole life."

I read the letter one more time before folding it to keep inside my pocket. I didn't tear it as I was not mad to tear such a beautiful, emotionally scripted letter.

I came down.

I used to come out to the roof at odd times and for no reasons other than to read the letter again and again, looking for any missed words or attempting to decipher some feelings hidden beneath those words, in a hope that it would reveal something new each time.

The mathematics tuition had been shifted to the morning hours, as most of the schools in Bokaro had announced their holidays.

Summer had just started and the temperature had risen a lot. The temperature was nearly about forty-five degrees. On that day, I didn't bring an umbrella also so I had no other choice than to walk quickly to the flat. Everyone was sleeping when I reached the flat.

In the evening, I had physics tuition. This schedule was on for the entire summer – Morning maths class and evening physics tuition.

I went to tuition; as usual tuition had been suspended. I waited for her. After five minutes, I spotted her coming on the scooty. Ritika was behind her. A smile flickered across my face. I moved ahead. She parked her scooty and came towards me. We strolled a little aside and we walked and talked for almost half an hour, holding hands.

"How was the letter?" she asked.

"It was lovely. I read it five times," I said without looking at her.

She laughed, "I knew it."

"Ashima, when will we start talking at night again?" I asked after a brief silence. She didn't respond. After some time, she left.

I didn't want to let her go, but when Ritika came, she went. I always asked her to stop for five more minutes, but she never listened.

On another day, when we met again, I asked, "I am going home today. Why didn't you call me at night? It has been ten days after that incident." I was a little impatient. "Even you leave early. I ask you every time to spare more time, but you never listen."

Tension had suddenly wrapped the environment. I said with discomfort, "You never feel sad about how bad I feel. How desperate I am for you."

She didn't say anything. Then Ritika came, and said, "Ashima, we should go. Chandrima's papa came and saw us. He also knew that today there is no tuition. And he is heading towards home. I am sure he will call our parents," she said hurriedly, "Sit behind me."

"Aarush, I am going," Ashima said.

"Don't go. Please, you do not even call me. Spare a few more minutes," I pleaded. "Please, don't go away now." I felt a frantic sense of desertion. Ritika was looking intently at me.

After a few seconds, Ashima moved forward and sat behind Ritika. I remained frozen. Now my anger rose. I took out that love letter and tore it to pieces and threw it on the ground.

There was silence. She looked at me.

Ritika started the scooty and was about to move. On seeing this, she said to Ritika, "Stop for a moment," and turned to me, "You should'nt have done this." Her voice rose. Her eyes flashed indecently.

"Ritika, move. I don't want to spend a moment here," she said in an aggravated tone. They left.

I started running, "Please don't go away. I am sorry. Sorry. Ashima... Ashima... stop... stop... for five minutes at least." But they didn't stop and left. I never felt this and a shock of realization made my body go numb. I stood there till they disappeared.

I left for Bokaro station at night; Firoz was with me. Holidays were declared in the tuition. We had a train at 10 p.m. and reached an hour early. I was still annoyed, not replying to any question Firoz was asking while coming to the station.

The train was on time. We didn't have reserved seats as we had to change the train from the next station, after one hour. We travelled in local class. It was crowded. We managed to somehow get a seat.

After half an hour, my phone vibrated and it was her call.

"Hello," I said.

"Hello, Aarush?"

"Yeah," I said in a low voice.

"Today, you behaved very badly. Tore the letter and threw it on the ground," her tone rose with anger. All the sweetness had vanished.

"Then what should I do? You don't even call me. It has been ten days since we have talked during the nights. I missed those talks, and you don't spend time with me either. You always walk away early," I said, in despair. I came near the gate. The noise of the train was deafening. So I came in the bathroom and locked the door.

"Then, what do I do? You never understand. You think everything should go according to you. You want me to go to mom and ask for the mobile and if she asks for a reason, then I should say that I have to talk to my boyfriend? You don't know, but it has been difficult. Every night, mummy comes and checks my room. Even if I talk to Tulika, she comes closer to me and listens to what am I talking about. I don't even talk to Tulika," she almost started screaming and shouting. Each time, her voice grew louder than before.

"Then, how are you calling today?" I broke my patience.

"Aarush, I know you suspect me. You think I deliberately don't call you. You are so mean. I called you because you got angry in the evening. I thought by calling, you will be happy. I took the phone by saying that I have to make an urgent call and closed the door. And you are saying like this." she said. I could easily sense the lump in her throat.

"But you act in such a way to make me feel hopeless. You also don't know or never tried to feel how am I living, without your calls, without hearing your voice and the good night kisses," I blurted out, trying to make her realize how badly I was missing her.

"Aarush, you think only about yourself. You never tried to think about me, about my condition. You think about yourself. Now, I am hanging up," And the phone went dead instantly.

I realized my mistakes, but I couldn't live without her. I called back. She didn't pick up the phone. I called again.

"What?" She picked up the phone after three rings.

"Don't do this. Don't disconnect the phone. Please talk to me. It is impossible to live without you. I am sorry," I sobbed in a squeaking tone. I felt that my face was enveloped in tingling frost.

She was silent on the other side of the line. After a brief silence, she said. "You wish that after all this I talk to you nicely like before, meet you when you want. It's not possible. It will take more time. Moreover, if I do anything wrong, we will not able to talk ever. You really hurt me. You are mean, so mean." The last line was a rising, wavering wail. "I am hanging up. I don't want to talk to you. You are very mean."

Before I could utter anything, the phone went dead.

I called back, but it was switched off. I was still inside the bathroom.

I was nauseated by the stench, a bloody stench. I called again. It started ringing.

"Sorry janu, don't do this. Please talk to me nicely. I will never do this again. It is impossible for me to live without you. I don't want to think of a minute without you," I squeaked with an imploring tone as she picked up the phone.

"Please, I don't want to talk to you. Please don't call me now. Mummy might come. Please don't call me," she said. It seemed that she even didn't hear what I had said. Suddenly, the phone went dead. I pressed the call button, but the screen didn't flash anything.

"Oh shit! Battery dead," I bellowed.

I stood there for a moment before someone knocked the door. I opened the door. It was Firoz.

"What are you doing here in the bathroom? You don't want to go home? We have reached the station," he said in surprise.

"Yeah," I sounded low, and I came out. Now, I needed some fresh air. I stood for a moment after coming out of the train on the platform. I gasped for a long time, inhaling a lot of fresh air.

The next train was nearly twenty minutes late. I sat with Firoz and he didn't ask me anything. I was silent, thinking about her. Her reaction saddened me terribly. I didn't even realize when the train arrived.

"Let's go. We have to talk to the ticket-checker to get us a seat."

He moved. I couldn't even sense his departure. I sat there, thinking of her reaction.

"Aarush, let's go. Train is about to leave the station. What are you doing here?" He came running and asked me.

"Yeah, sorry. Let's go," I said, coming to my senses. I moved along with him.

It was a bad night for us. We didn't get a seat. We travelled the whole night standing near the gate, but managed to reach home.

"I am going to sleep," Firoz said to me after coming out of Siwan station.

I nodded. My sleep had been taken away. My mind was still wandering over her. Till now, I hadn't got her call.

I reached home and told my mother that I was home for five days. I didn't get her call for two days.

On the second night, I went to sleep after making the bed. I stretched myself on the bed. It was very hot. The temperature was nearly about thirty-eight degrees. It was a moonlit night. Moon was shining, delivering its light, coming down dimly. There was no breeze at all and the atmosphere seemed stale. It made the situation worse. Due to some problem at the electric pole, there was no chance of power for the whole night which made the situation terrible. I was continuously shaking the hand-fan. The whole body was drenched in the sweat, but I didn't care about this. I held the phone in my hand, gazing over it and hoping for a call. But it seemed I was hoping against hope. I slid the phone under the pillow, said in a soft whisper, "I love you Ashima. I love you very much." And I tried to sleep.

After some time, I suddenly woke up, picked up the phone and checked. Three missed calls. A faint smile crawled across my face. Sleep drifted away from my eyes. I called back. It was ringing. I stood up and sat.

"Hello," I said, as she picked up the phone a moment later. "I was sleeping, so I couldn't pick up the phone."

She was silent; even she didn't utter a reply. After a moment she said, "I can't talk to you. I called you, but you didn't pick up the phone," she said. It seemed that all her sweetness had evaporated. It was unpleasant to hear this.

"I am sorry. Don't do this. I told you I was sleeping. I didn't expect the call as you hadn't called me for two days. Why won't you talk to me? Why are you doing this? I am sorry that I couldn't pick up the phone." I was surprised with her behaviour.

"Didi has come. She is with me, in my room. She had gone out so I picked up your phone," she said.

"Don't do this. Please. Please. I haven't talked to you for two days. Please," I pleaded.

"I don't know. I am hanging up the phone. Bye," she said in a harsh tone and the phone went dead.

I immediately called her back. She disconnected the phone. I called continuously five times and every time shedid the same. I called again only to hear, "The number you are trying to reach is switched off." I was sad and angry. I started weeping. I wept the whole night. I called thrice during that night; twice it the phone was switched off, but once it rang but she disconnected the phone and switched off the mobile.

The whole of the next day, I waited for her call. But I didn't get the call. I kept the phone in my hand the whole day. Even when mummy asked for it, I lied. I lied each time she asked me.

That night, I didn't sleep. I was waiting for her call. It was eleven in the night and still no call from her. I was a bit sleepy, but I didn't want to miss the chance of picking her call, so I splashed my eyes with some water.

It was a dark night; I slept in the room. She called me at midnight.

"Hello, I was waiting for your call. If I would have slept then you would had said the same thing as you did last night so I was waiting for you to call," I said in a whisper with a small smile on my face.

"But I can't talk to you. I don't have balance," she said, but it sounded like a lie.

"Don't worry, I will call you." I had balance, but was cautious as my father was strict and checked my balance. I didn't want to miss a chance to talk to her. I thought over this for a while and I called back.

"Hello," I said, hiding my problem.

"Hello," she said. I could hear the lack of energy in her voice.

"Last night, I called you back," I had barely spoken any words and she bellowed from the other side.

"Again, you are thinking of yourself. I told you didi was there but you have to talk only, nothing more. You don't try to understand the other's problem."

"I am sorry, if you think like that. I just asked," I said slowly. I didn't want to spend time quarrelling and shouting, but this time too I couldn't complete my sentence and she shouted again. This time I had to lower the volume of mobile phone.

"What did you just ask me?" she questioned.

I didn't know what to do, what to ask and what to say. I was listening to her quietly and calmly. I knew if I said anything, she would switch off the mobile.

"You are shouting because of me. I am really sorry," I could manage to say this. "What were you doing?" I asked, trying to divert her.

"Nothing," came the short reply.

I was still confused about why she was doing this. I always wished to live a peaceful life, a sweet life, a life full of love. I never wanted to see her behave in this way. A silence hovered. She was silent. So was I. I tried to calm my agitation.

"I am hanging up," she said.

"Why? We could talk. It has been days since we spoke nicely," I protested softly with a whisper. I didn't want to keep the phone, "Please talk to me."

"No, I am putting down the phone." Her voice was dry and charmless. She hung up the phone before I could continue and stop her.

I called her back. She picked up and said in an acerbic tone, "What?"

I hesitated to say anything, and kept silent.

"If you have to say anything, and then say it, otherwise I'll keep the phone down."

I gave a moan in despair. I heard a click, and I knew that the phone had gone dead.

I called back, but my heart was filled with despair when I heard that the phone had been switched off. I checked the balance. Thirty-seven rupees had gone out. I threw my phone and I didn't know when I slept off.

"Aarush, Aarush, wake up!" my father shouted.

"What? Please let me sleep," I murmured in a sleepy tone.

"There is Rs 63 balance. But it was Rs 100," he said. I saw him frowning. I knew this was going to happen, so I had thought of an idea the previous night.

I woke up, yawned and said, "I don't know. It was hundred rupees but when I checked before sleeping, it was Rs 63. I even called the customer care; they told that it was a mistake and they will rebalance it till noon," I glibly lied.

"But it has never happened before," my father said and kept the phone on the table and left the room. I heaved a sigh of relief.

I woke up and went directly to the ATM. I took out the last hundred rupee note which I thought I would use to buy a book, but I had no other option than to recharge the cell phone. I recharged the phone with a hundred rupees coupon.

I didn't get a call for the next two days. I was impatient and angry with her behaviour. My anger always evaporated when the pang of memories, lovely memories, her sweet voice, her 'I love yous' stabbed me.

I decided to return to Bokaro. "Mummy, tomorrow, I am going back," I said, packing my bag.

I called Tulika in the evening. She picked up the phone after four rings.

"Hello." She chuckled with a childish tone.

"Hello, you seem to be very happy. What is the matter?" I asked.

"Nothing great. I am alone at home, means me and my sibling," she said and giggled happily again.

"Why? Where are your parents?" I asked.

"Both mummy and papa have gone to London. And they will be back by next week. You know Aarush, what I miss the most in my life?" she said as her voice shifted to a moan.

I was silent and listening, and murmured, "What?"

"You know, my parents never have time for us. They are always busy with their work. I wish my parents would spend some time with me like others' parents do. You know, they provided me with everything, whatever I wish for. But I don't want these things. I want their love and their time," she said. Her pain was intense; I sensed it and became silent.

"Hey, pagli, mad girl, it's not like that. They really love you. No parents wish a life like this, but they also have their own problems. They are doing this for you only, for your happiness, so that their children can live a happy life, a life where there is no place for discomfort," I assured her. I heard a sob. "Don't weep. Why are you feeling like this? We are with you every moment."

"So sweet. You are really very sweet and caring. Oh, leave it. So you are talking with Ashima? I know there's a problem, but—"

I interrupted, "What should I say? We are hardly talking and she is behaving very rudely. She is not talking to me. She calls whenever she wishes and switches off the phone after a minute. I don't understand why she is doing this? And—" and before I could say anymore, I saw my brother coming towards me. "I will call you later," I whispered.

"Why? What happened?" She was shocked.

"Bye... bye," I whispered as my brother came and stood beside me, barely a fifteen inches away. He looked at me with suspicion as I could see his eyes narrowing. I saw that he lowered his eyes to hear to whom I was talking to. I pretended that I was still talking after hanging up on Tulika. "Hello, Ritesh. When? Tomorrow? Okay, I will come. Bye."

Next day, I left Siwan for Bokaro. I was alone as the others were coming over the weekend. I reached Bokaro in the morning, around 5 o' clock.

17

The summer heat spread across the streets. Bokaro has a steel plant, and it might be the reason for this rise in temperature. As the mess was closed and would start only from the next day, I had to go out, though it was unbearable. I had no energy to leave the room, but I was too hungry. Lot of things was packed in my bag. I checked it. There were three small bags; one had bhujiya and some other some snacks. I ate some snacks, some namkeen, bhujiya and biscuits.

Then my phone vibrated. I left that snack-bag on the table and picked up the phone, "Hello."

It was Ashima. She said in a tickled tone, "Hello, when are you coming?"

First I thought that I should lie, but after a brief silence, I said, "I am in Bokaro."

"What?"

"I came back today morning," I said slowly.

"But you didn't tell me," she grumbled. Her voice was louder than usual.

"How could I? You hadn't called me for a single time since Friday," I said.

She was silent; might have been the silence of guilt.

"Okay, I am hanging up." Her tone was calmer than earlier. I didn't say anything. I didn't even plead to her to keep talking. And she cut the phone.

The whole flat was silent. The silence conquered the streets too. A very few day scholars were present.

I was nervous about her behavior. I didn't do anything the whole day; did not even unpack my bag. It had been a month since I had talked to her properly. I was pondering over the same issue daily.

It was nearly 10:45 p.m. I dozed off on my bed when my phone vibrated. It was Ashima.

I picked up, "Hello."

No reply.

"Hello," I said again and sat on the bed.

I was a little surprised over this because I heard a sob, a hissing sob. Before I could say anymore, she broke into tears. She wept for a long time and didn't utter a word. After sometime, I heard a few murmurs with hisses. I wasn't able to understand. I was surprised and confused over this and a moment later, my shock merged into curiosity when I heard a fragile sorry "*S. .. o... o... r... y!*"

"What happened?" I was numb with discomfort and I wasn't able to understand what was going on or what had happened. "What happened? Did anyone scold you? Please tell me. For god's sake, I don't like it when you weep like this."

My heartbeat had become rapid when she didn't utter a single word except a fragile sorry which was coming out with a wail. I didn't know what to say, except try to soothe her.

Her cry slackened after a minute and she said in a slower tone, still whispering, "I am sorry Aarush. I am really sorry."

"Sorry... why?" I asked with amazement. "And please don't say sorry. It really sounds awkward, especially when you say it."

"Aarush, I am really sorry. I am sorry for what I did to you," she said, raising her voice a little.

"But you didn't do anything wrong," I said.

"No, I did. I hurt you. I hurt you with my behaviour, with my tone. I didn't talk to you nicely. You called me so many times, but I didn't answer your call. Every time I switched the phone off. I am very bad, very bad. You tried to talk nicely, but I never did. I should have understood your feelings. You tried to talk to me when your father came to meet you, but I—"

I interrupted, "Please don't feel this way. For me, what could be better than the fact that you came back with the same love and care? I don't want anything except this. I always wish that we'd talk nicely throughout our life."

I was happy. I thanked Tulika. I knew she must have told something to her so that she realized her guilt.

"Aarush, please forgive me," she said.

"Oh, never say this. In fact, I always forced you to call me, even after knowing everything," I said softly in an appeasing way, "Now, everything has become good. Now, we will talk nicely. It has been a month that we have said the three magic words and have exchanged lovely kisses. She replied with a soothing, "I love you".

And lots of kisses which made me smile. But this smile evaporated when she said, "Aarush, I will have to go now because of didi. She will go after three days, then we will talk for long, for the whole night."

This was what I didn't like. But I had no option but to be calm and say nothing. I didn't want to make her angry again.

"Hmm. But call me when you get time," I said half mindedly.

She hung up with a whisper of sorry and I love you.

I didn't get her call for two days. Not even a single message. I was annoyed. Every hour I used to check the phone, and my veins hurt to see a blank screen. "All that happened that night was a drama – typical drama. All the apologies, all that crying, everything was just drama." I felt annoyed and frustrated, extremely uncomfortable with the situation I was in.

4th June 2007

The heat from the sun had almost burnt Bokaro, penetrating the very flesh of the people. The rooms and beds were too warm. I came from outside and was drenched in sweat. Sitting down, I opened my lunch box.

"Oh! A missed call," I whispered as I picked up the phone. Two missed calls. It was Tulika.

I called back.

"Hello, hi!" I said, wiping the sweat off my forehead. My handkerchief itself had been wet through that drops of sweat could be wrung out.

"Hello. Where are you? Can you come to the city center?" She said. I heard the voice of Aachanky whisper from the back.

"Where?"

"Near the Harshwardhan Plaza, at its entrance," she said.

"Ok, I am coming. Wait for five minutes," I said and put the phone down. I knew the presence of Ashima would drive me anywhere, maybe even out of this world.

I hadn't even finished my lunch. I hurriedly packed the lunch box, picked up the cycle and headed to city center in the same hollow-eyed, dishevelled and exhausted state. I reached there in five minutes. I parked the cycle near the stand and looked around. No sign of her. I saw them after a few minutes, coming from the other side. They had two or three shopping bags with them. Ashima was smiling, Tulika too. I smiled a fake one.

"Shopping?" I whispered keeping a smile on face.

"Yeah, clothes and all those things. You know Ashima bought a skirt – a mini one and a top, a short top," she said, with a teasing voice and smiling widely. "You know she also bought two br—"

"Tulika, please stop it now. Please!" Ashima interrupted, nudging her.

I was silent and trying to interpret what Tulika wanted to say. I was smiling, but my eyes retained a look of solemnity.

Tulika started laughing loud.ly Ashima gave me a coy smile.

Ashima came nearer and showed me her dress, a pink skirt – a brown flecked one with a pinkish design in the center. She also showed me the bangles – red, blue and green.

"Nice, it's lovely," I said. I concealed my lack of interest. "Such a lovely colour especially the top. Baby pink suits you the most."

"Why did not you call me for the past two days?" I almost shouted when I finally lost my patience.

Ashima looked at Tulika and Tulika walked away from us.

"You start shouting in front of everyone. You should know that Tulika is there. What will she think?" she said softly and feeling awkward, a grimace on her face.

I realized my mistake. I lowered my tone and said, "Why didn't you call me for two days? I was waiting. You know very well that I feel frustrated about this."

She was silent for a moment, then began saying, "Actually, didi is there. So I was not able to call you. I tried so many times but, she was always around."

"You didn't call me for two days. You know how much I wanted to talk to you. It has been more than a month that we talked nicely," I said, raising my tone. "I am not coming to tuition today."

"Why? Why you are not coming?" she said softly and urged with a sweet expression which so often caused me to smile but it looked cloying. "I will call you. Sure."

"No, I am not coming. If you are bad, then I am also bad."

"Aarush, I don't know, you are coming to the tuition. If you will not come, I am not going to call you," she retorted in a teasing voice.

I didn't know what, but I noticed something peculiar in her eyes. I sensed the absence of love, which I used to see before, that glint of love.

Tulika came after some time, so we both went quiet.

"I hope you have had your talk," Tulika said with a smile. A distressed look passed over.

I smiled and nodded.

"Ashima, we should go now. It is quite late," Tulika said to her.

I looked at her with anguish and nodded in a disapproving way. I turned towards the cycle stand.

I was so angry that I didn't go to the tuition that evening. My heart couldn't still bear the stupid act I had done. I always missed her, but my ego – for the first time – didn't allow me to go. I don't really have an inflated ego, but this time, I forced myself to show some attitude. As time passed, my patience broke down, and my anguish vanished. I came out to the balcony to check whether the boys were coming or not so that I could go and meet her. My patience broke. I waited for five minutes before I could see a boy who was with me in the tuition. I hurriedly went into the room and put on a t-shirt and my pants. My phone vibrated.

"Hello, had you came to the tuition?" It was Ashima calling from Ritika's number that she used to call from earlier. I thought I'd lie first, but I could not. "No." My voice was austere.

"Good," she said harshly and disconnected the phone.

When nothing came to my mind, I thought of surprising her.

"I know she is angry. I must surprise her. She must be there," I thought and rushed towards the tuition. I chose the other road, running parallel to the tuition road.

Her scooty ensured me of her presence. But she was not near the tuition gate. No one was there, not even Ritika and Divya. I moved ahead to catch a sight of her. The tuition staff waved at me and asked, "Why didn't you come for the class?"

I nodded but didn't say anything. My eyes were looking for her.

On the other side of tuition, near the newly constructed buildings, I saw her. My heart got plunged. She was surrounded by three to four boys, standing very close to them. Divya was also there. I could not see who they were but there were a total of four boys. I felt crippled. I noticed that one boy was very close to her and whispering something, and she was smiling gaily. I tried to hide, but I couldn't do so, as Divya and Ashima saw me the next moment. My heart started to beat faster, increasing with every second. The shock of realization made my face go numb. A violent shiver shook me. I felt my feet frozen to the earth. I couldn't believe that she was talking to them in such a familiar manner. I blinked painfully in the blinding glare. "The girl whom I trusted so much, whom I love so much and cared for so much does such things behind my back! It meant she did these things after every class in my absence. Oh my god, that's why she waited after tuition was over," I thought.

My mind was reeling over these things. I found it almost impossible to believe. I was on the verge of breaking into tears when Divya looked at me and said something to Ashima, who turned to look at me and turned again and started talking to them. I felt a frantic sense of desertion.

I called Tulika.

"Tulika, see! Ashima is talking to some boys. She even looked at me, but she didn't come. Why is she doing this?" I said in a melancholic manner.

"Aarush, please don't stand there. Come back, I request you," Tulika said. She sensed the problem.

"How? How could she do this?" I sensed that I had enormous difficulty in getting the words out and I broke down into tears.

"Aarush, I urge you to go back. Don't just stand there," she urged. Suddenly, the phone went dead. The talk time was over.

Ashima was still talking to them in the same cavorting way. She wore the same new skirt and top that I had seen in the afternoon. My face contorted in lamentation and pain.

It was now a thing of mingled bereavement and anxiety, and bewilderingly intense. The waves of fearful cramps made me stand there for minutes. I found the betrayer of my trust in front of my eyes. When it became unbearable to see this, I moved forward slowly.

After moving a few meters, she came on her scooty and stood in front of me. "Aarush, listen!"

I avoided her and moved ahead. She again came and stood in front me, "Aarush, please listen." My nerves flamed with anger.

"What should I listen to? You don't need to explain anything to me. I saw everything, your every act in my absence. I understood what you do after the tuition gets over. You never go home after tuition. And I go home and you do this. This is a betrayal of my trust," I almost shouted at her. I was too angry to talk and thus managed to tell her, "Please go home. I don't want to talk to you right now. You don't know how angry I am right now."

"No, they came today itself. Trust me. They have never come before. Trust me. And I didn't come to the tuition because I wanted you to feel how bad I felt when you didn't come. They are my old friends. They even told me to go away when they saw you," she said with a quiver in her voice.

My face was even more twisted and tormented than before now. A twinge of anger passed all through my veins and I couldn't control it. Finally, I lost mobility for a second and shouted "Friends? Huh! Friends?

She began to babble a bit, but my shout warned her to stop. And she did.

"They are your friends. No, you do this daily in my absence. I know. They are your friends and you talk to your friends in a cavorting way. Why don't you strip in front them and then talk?" I blurted out. I pronounced these words as I was unaware of its exact resonance. I didn't know what I had said a second earlier. I had lost complete control over my mind and tongue. In anger, a man loses his wisdom and he doesn't know how to react. And same happened with me. The people passing by looked at both of us, and tried to enquire what was going on.

She was shocked and appalled when she heard me. Her pupils dilated in shock. She had begun to weep. The tears spilled down her cheeks.

There was a huge and troubling space around us after this. She became silent. I realized what I had said was wrong – utterly wrong, and before I could speak further, she said, "Aarush, you are really mean, very very bad. I won't talk to you ever after this." And she left, weeping.

I saw her going away from me, away from my life. At this instant, I sensed for the first time that a distance was separating us, an intolerable distance. Each ticking moment seemed to take Ashima away from me. I stood there, seeing her fading away from my sight, maybe away from my life. My love was fading away.

My anger evaporated soon. Then, I realized my mistake. I came back to hostel heavy footed.

At night, I didn't get her call. I impatiently called Tulika.

"Hello, please tell her to call me once," I said almost in a begging tone, without hearing her hello. "Please! I cannot live without her. I want to say sorry. I was angry and I didn't say it deliberately. You know how much I love her."

Tulika told me that Ashima had left for Delhi due to the sudden demise of her maternal uncle.

◆

"Hey, what's up? Ashima, a girl with whom you are hooked up. I know everything," Varun started to tease me as I sat next to him.

"Who told you these things?" I said in a jocular tone, trying not to get excited. "How do you know these things?"

"No, first tell me that are you hooked up with her?" he said.

"I was," I said and faded in melancholy.

"Was? What do you mean? I really don't understand," he said with amazement.

"Leave it; just tell me how do you know about me?" I asked.

"You would know. A boy, her friend. He told me about you. He is also a good friend of hers."

"Who? I don't know. Is he from Bokaro?" I said, first amazed then frowning in anger.

"How could you not know? He is from Gaya. He has been a friend, a good friend, for more than a year," he said.

"Who is it? I don't know." I was on the verge of breaking down.

"His name is Shauryadeep. You might have heard his name."

"No, I have never heard about him. Tell me something more," I said. My eyes dilated with anguish and pain.

"I don't know much about them. Actually, if you don't mind, I would say I don't like that girl," he said firmly.

"Could I meet him?" I said.

"Yeah, sure."

Next day in the evening, we went to sector 4B. Varun called him. He came out.

"Meet Aarush, you know," Varun said to him.

"Hello!" he said and flapped his hand before me amiably.

"Hello," I said firmly but in a slower tone. "For how long have you been friends with Ashima? And who extended the hand of friendship first?"

"Since last January. At the time of her birthday. She did," he said.

"What? How did you come to know about her birthday? Do you both talk on phone?"

"She came to me and forcibly asked me to wish her. She told me about you that you are a very good person. Yeah, we talk on the phone. I asked for her number."

I interrupted, "And she gave it to you?" My heart ached with pain. I gave him a penetrating look.

"Yeah. She warned me that unless she gave me a missed call, I should not call her. She gives me a missed call and I call her. Sometimes, she calls me. We often talk in the night, around 11 p.m."

Oh, its means she doesn't talk to her didi. She's been talking to you, I thought. I was appalled to hear this. "Anything else?"

He followed with a sigh, touched with melancholy. I sensed I was about to hear something more unusual. My heart started pounding.

"I have seen her talking to others boys also. We even meet in the canteen. In fact, she talked to every boy in the school, even with Deependra. I told her most time not to talk to them, but she never listened. On the day, when your dad came and you were calling, her phone was busy; at that time, she was talking to me. She told me that you were calling and I asked her to talk to you. She said that she would say that she was talking to her sister. And she was confident that you wouldn't ask any questions as you trusted her."

My heart gave a tumultuous lurch. I shut my eyes tightly and pursed my lips in pain. I realize that my eyes filled with tears and throat choked with sobs.

I moved forward to unlock my cycle.

"Where are you going?" Varun shouted.

"I can't hear this. My heart is breaking. I am going."

I couldn't hear anymore. I left that place as rapidly as I could. I was on the verge of crying. My eyes filled with tears. It seemed someone had slapped me on my face, hard. Tears started streaming down. His each word about her had stabbed me.

I never met them after this. I broke all contact with them. I even changed the batch of my maths tuition.

18

I could no longer sleep. A wistful pain swept through my heart. "How could she do this? She had cheated on me. She made fun of my loyalty, my love. She traded my goodness and played with it." I didn't know what to do; except wiping off the tears.

"I loved her so much. Though I've pleaded with her, said sorry many times. She is stone-hearted," I wept. I had nothing to do but cover my face with a pillow to hide it from others. Shauryadeep's words echoed in my mind over and over.

Firoz was not in the room.

I picked out my lockable-diary from the suitcase; it was at the bottom, amid some shirts. I unlocked it and turned the first page. A heart – big, red coloured, pierced with an arrow – was drawn on which was written our names together. I turned the pages, ignoring that. Those words I'd written were more than well-narrated literature to me. I just held the diary in my hand, merely glancing at a random phrase. With each word, I felt her presence more. Suddenly I stopped as I saw our names together on the right pages. How sweet it was! It seemed someone had kept their heart out on the paper. On the left, the page was blank, with a written heading: "*Janu, aap apna photo lagana.*" I felt a wave of nostalgia and I started talking to myself, "Please Ashima, come back to me. Please forgive me. I can't live without you." Every letter in the diary started stroking me and those flashes were as sweet and salty as my tears. I could easily hear the choking sob in my throat.

From time to time, I uttered, "Please come back. Please forgive me." I arose, came near the window. The air blew and I turned the pages, still the tears began rolling off my eyes. On the left was a picture of Ashima and the right one was blank, subscripted, 'Stick your photo. And see how beautiful and nice we look together.'

The light was switched off. Door was closed. I was alone. The road was silent and dark, like the room. I gazed fixedly into the gloom, the silence, the darkness on the road was mirroring my life and I broke into a wail. I also didn't know how I long was there, standing silently and weeping. Tears were streaming down continuously and slipping down the cheeks. I even forgot to wipe them. The knock on the door broke my silence. I wiped my tears, first with my hand then with a towel. I put on the light and put a fake smile on my face before opening the door.

It was Firoz.

◆

Next day, I went to the tuition. My eyes were looking for her, but there was sign of her. I sat sulking and desolate on the last bench.

It had been six days since she had left her Bokaro.

Next day, I reached the tuition early. I saw her standing next to Divya.

I became happy and a ray of hope flushed in my heart. I moved fast to the class centre. She looked at me once, but in a sullen and pensive way.

All the students started entering the classroom, but I stood there, waiting for her to go. My eyes dilated with confusion at her avoidance when she passed me without casting a glance at me. My heart ached. I followed her. On the staircase, I put my hand on her shoulder. She turned and brushed off my hand. For the first time, I saw a different shade other than love and adoration in her eyes; it was something strange. There was no longer happiness on her face, no pink blush on her lips. My heart panged and I understood she was very angry with me. Now, she must have started hating me. This made me feel that our breakup was near and my heart started wobbling up and down.

I didn't say anything. She also entered the class without uttering a word. I sat alone and isolated on the last bench. I kept looking at her in the whole class and was waiting for tuition to get over eagerly.

To my surprise, she came out of the tuition and went away without looking at me. I saw her till she vanished at the next turning street.

I stood there forlorn and desolate. I tried to shout, but my voice got stuck in my throat. I called Tulika.

"Hello," I said, little bit impatiently.She greeted me and I continued, "Tulika, see. She came to tuition but she did not even look at me. She avoided me. I want to say sorry to her. You know, it has been so long that I haven't talked to her."

"I know she came back in the morning. She is still angry. Look, Aarush, it will be better not to talk to her. Give her some time. Maybe after some time she will call you?" she interrupted with a cold and calm tone.

"But, you know, I can't live without her, without talking to her. I want to hear her voice. Please tell her to call me. At least once, at least she should listen to what I have to say."

Someone from behind called me and I put down the phone. It was Ritika.

"Hi, Aarush. What happened? Why are you looking so lost?" Ritika said.

"Ashima went away without talking to me; she didn't even look at me," I said sadly. My lips became dry.

"I saw. She has become so heartless. I was noticing that since the moment when she came down as I was with her. I once talked about you to her, but avoided the topic," she said. "But don't be sad. I will talk to her again."

"Thanks," I mumbled and strolled away.

◆

Days passed. I tried everything to talk to her. I once called her on her land line, but her mummy picked up the phone. It had been a month since I talked to her. Each time, I caught a glimpse of her fathomless eyes, my heart gave a savage lunge. I wanted to re-establish face to face conversation, eye to eye contact, our mutual love, our loving relationship, but hopes were slim. And I was devastated. Each passing second, minute and day were taking away Ashima. I felt crippled now. Even Tulika didn't call me or talk to me.

I started bunking classes. I stayed in the room feeling quiet and adrift. I stopped talking to anyone except Ritika, sometimes, only about her.

School reopened. But I was not going to the classes. It had been five days. Ritika called me to know why I was not coming to school.

I was silent. I knew she cared for me. After a brief silence, I murmured, "Did you talk to her? What did she say? Will she come back to me?" Agitation edged my voice.

She was silent and her silence scared my heart. Further few seconds, she didn't speak. And my heart raced on and I continued with anxiety, "What did she say? Say something."

"I talked to her, but she doesn't wish to talk to you. She said she hates you. She doesn't even want to see you. But Aarush, you need not worry. I will force her to talk to you... at least once."

With every word, my heart settled down. Her words stabbed me. I gave a moan of despair.

"Aarush, I empathize. But you should be optimistic about your relationship and you should not feel this way. Everything will be fine. One day, she will realize."

"Optimistic! A bleak optimistic! You know, she wants to leave me. She doesn't want me any longer. And she got a chance for a break-up," I objected in a whisper, thinking negatively for the first time. Tears started streaming down and my voice .

"Aarush, you should not feel this way. She will be back with you," she tried to calm my agitation. "And please don't cry. Please come to school. You know life indeed goes on. Otherwise, you will have nothing at last. Take care of yourself."

My head was bursting with a headache, an uncontrollable headache. I said in a faint voice, "I have a headache. I am hanging up the phone."

"Aarush, take care of yourself," she said. Before she could say anything, I disconnected the phone.

I slipped onto a chair. I had never felt such pain ever in my head. It was bursting. It was unbearable. So I slept.

A knock on the door woke me up. Headache was still there, but little a better this time. I checked the time. It was six in the evening.

I opened the door. It was Varun.

"Hey, how are you? You are not coming to the maths class. So I came to know the reason. Are you okay?" He asked on seeing my dried, parched face. "Bhaiya was asking about you."

"I am fine," I replied. "I had a headache, so I was sleeping."

"I know you are lying. Did anything happen? Did she call you? Did you talk to her? You know everyone in the school is talking about your relationship.

"No, she doesn't want to talk to me. I don't know what to do now."

He was surprised and angry at her insensitive attitude. He became silent and looked at me. There was silence. It prevailed over more than five minutes.

"Hey, I have a plan. We will pretend you've tried to suicide."

"What?" The idea sounded preposterous. "Don't you think it is ridiculous? It will bruise my relationship. Moreover, she will become angrier," I shook my head disappointedly.

"No, look. I will message Tulika that you have cut your veins and I will say that I am your roommate. As I reached home after tuition, I saw your hand was bleeding."

I knew this was ridiculous but I hadn't any better idea than this. After thinking for a few seconds, I nodded.

Varun wrote an SMS from my mobile and sent it to Tulika.

"Tulika, Aarush has cut the veins of his hand. Now, he is okay as I saw him unconscious after coming from tuition. I called the doctor. I am his roommate."

We waited for a reply for the next half an hour, but didn't get any.

"I know she is not going to reply. She has nothing to do with me or with my condition," I said, looking disappointed.

Varun remained silent. He was also puzzled. After a moment, he said, "Aarush, maybe she does not have her phone. I can surely say she will reply."

Soon he left and said, "Take care."

My head was bursting with pain, and Firoz hadn't come yet. So I slept again.

When I woke up, I checked my mobile phone. Two missed calls. And a message. Hurriedly, I checked. One missed call was from Tulika and the other was from my father. I opened the message. It was sent by Tulika.

Message reads:

"Aarush, have you become crazy? How could you do this? Have you become mad? How are you? I am calling Ashima now to tell her this."

I deleted this message. My phone vibrated again. A new message. It was from Tulika again.

"Aarush, I called Ashima. She was worried to hear this. But she can't call you now. She will call you tomorrow. May be in the noon. You wait and don't do anything silly. Take care of yourself."

I felt a sigh of relief. My headache disappeared completely after reading this.

The next day, I was waiting for her phone impatiently. I got her call, as expected, at around noon. It was like a ray, of hope in the dark, cold room.

"Hello!" I was hearing her almost after a month.

"Why did you do this? If anything had happened to you then, how you are now?" Her voice was normal. It felt good to know she worried for me. What should I answer to this question? I had lied." I thought.

"I am fine now. Ashima, I am sorry for what I did. Please come back. I feel lonely without you," I said in a pleading tone, after a brief pause.

She didn't say anything for a while. "Aarush, I want my diary back."

"No, I will not give it to you. You know, this is the only thing of you which is with me. I know you will not give it back," my words were fading away.

"Aarush, I will give it back," her tone was polite and at that instance, it was strange.

"No, I won't. You will not return it," I opposed.

"Aarush, if you will not give it, I will not come back to you ever," she said in a way that she would come to me if I give this diary to her.

"Please, Aarush. I will return it to you the very next day," she urged sweetly and my heart melted.

"Okay, I will give it to you, but you will return it in the next class," I said, my voice uttered gloomily. And as I said this, the phone got disconnected. I sensed something unusual.

The next day, I went to the tuition class with her diary. After the class got over, I came aside where we used to meet. She was already there with Divya.

I passed a look of contrition. But her face remained normal. Her look was no longer tender.

I passed the diary to her. She said nothing. After that, they walked away. A shudder passed through me. I found something peculiar. Her facial expression, tranquil and serene, had changed into cunning and heinous.

"How heartless she has become. She didn't talk to me," I thought as I watched her walking away. I stood there and another shudder passed; a current of sad bewilderment when I saw her smiling. My eyes narrowed and it seemed that she said to Divya, "Oh finally, I got this."

My heart ached each time when she behaved like a stranger. It lasted a moment in disbelief before it was replaced by something I called hate. I had nothing to do except to go away.

◆

I was waiting for Ritika impatiently. I got her message:

"She is back. Meet you in school."

Next day, all students went to the computer lab except a few. Ritika stayed with me. I explained everything.

"I know this entire thing," she said coldly.

"You know everything. How did you know these things? If you knew these things, why didn't you tell me? The diary was the last thing of her. There was her photo which I used to see daily. Now, it is also gone," I uttered. My throat started choking.

"I am sorry. She told these things when I was leaving for Ranchi. She told me after your apparent suicide act, she said that if you do anything unusual to yourself, and you have her diary, she would be in trouble. And she didn't want to entangle herself in any of these things. So, she tricked you to get out the diary from you. I am very sorry," she said, looking down. I sensed the soft tone of apology.

"What?"

Her words paralyzed me. I stood numb and expressionless.

"What else has she told you?" I asked. The words were barely coming out of my throat.

"Nothing," she said.

"Don't lie to me. I know you are lying."

After some time, Ritika said, "She said that you shout at her. You forced her not to talk to any boys. You put restrictions on her wearing tight tops and any short dresses."

"But she could have told all this to me directly."

She again continued after a brief halt, "She said that she was with you merely for time pass. She even talks to everyone behind you. You know, she chats with boys on the internet; a boy even proposed to her and sent his photo to her. Even after this, she continued chatting."

My look shifted from a puzzled one to a shocked, then to disappointment. My face changed, turned grave. My eyes watered and I was on the verge of crying.

"What?" I almost wailed.

"Yeah, but she also knows you love her much. She hadn't had any reason. Perhaps, you have shared your problems. She even said that you are not rich enough."

"But money problems had been sorted out at that time. She supported me then."

"Yeah, I know. No, she still thinks about this. She said to me that at that time, she had nothing to say except what she said. When you shouted at her on that day, she got a chance. She chose her friends over you. I tried many times to convince her that love always has to be kept before others. But I failed."

"How did she do this? How cunning she is! I said not to wear tight tops and short dresses only in tuition. I am possessive about her. I don't like when other students stare at her. That's why I said this. How did she think like this? You know what I read on the tables? How many times I erased those things. Vulgar things about her. How could I bear this? That's why I put some restrictions on her. You know how painful it was to read those things? I wanted to protect her from others, from those dirty eyes. How she could be so mean?" I said and tears started streaming down my cheeks. Words were trembling and barely coming out of my throat.

"Aarush, are you all right? Are you?" She shook my hands.

I didn't say anything for a long time. I was numb. When I tried, words were stammering one after the other. It seemed that a lump choked my throat. "She is so cheap. My love for her has become a problem for her. Somewhere, it's my fault."

"No, it is not your fault. She talked to others at night behind your back. She doesn't deserve you. I know you love her. I know what you did for your relationship to talk to her."

Her voice rose now, sauced with affirmation, "Aarush, forget her. Now, live life for yourself. Your whole life is still in front of you. You might not know that tomorrow brings more gifts, more happiness. You know my father says, if you envelop your face with a laugh, then there will be no place for crying, grief and sorrow. Life never guarantees happiness or sadness. It will soon fade away. And you will come back to the arms of happiness and fun."

I was silent and tears streamed down. The lights were fading. I wasn't able to think anything. My senses became numb. I had never imagined my life without her.

"Now, like a good boy, you will not cry. I am with you to support you. Don't talk to her ever." She wiped my tears. "Smile! A frail face also houses bad thinking and life. Smile!"

I gazed at her, at her soft spoken tone, at her tenderness. Because of her wishes, a hint of gratitude pushed a weak smile across my face.

"Thanks," I whispered. Her light-hearted words washed over me like cold rains. It relieved me. When one door closed, god always opened other doors too. Ritika was another door for me.

Just then, the bell rang. Students started coming to class. I didn't realize how the next two hours passed.

19

25 August 2007

Days went on. Ritika always called me to ask about me. Each time, she advised me to keep myself away from Ashima. I took Ritika's advice, and just nodded in acceptance.

I knew Ashima wouldn't talk to me. She even left tuition without telling me about it. It was unbearable, but she didn't know I went to tuition only for her.

In those following days, I scrambled frantically to commit it all to memory; like an art lover running out of a burning museum, I grabbed whatever I could – her look, a whisper, her glance, scraps of love, and shadows of golden days.

It was 11 p.m. when I was lost into thinking about her, when my phone vibrated. I wiped my tears. It was from Ashima. A strained and unworthy smile flickered across my face.

"Hello."

"Hello, what did you say to Shauryadeep? Tell me. You narrow minded person!" she shouted. Her tone was harsh and rough.

"Who is Shauryadeep?" I asked and said after a brief pause, "No, I didn't say anything. You never told me that you ever talked to anyone at night, except to your sister," I said politely.

Silence. I knew she had no answer for this.

"Is it because I am not coming back to you that you are spreading rumours? First to Ritika, then Varun, and now to

Shauryadeep? You narrow minded person. My father was right. He said that never make a friend from a small town. I never listened to him!" she was shouting, and my tears started rolling down. It wasn't easy tolerating her saying such things.

"Why are you saying like this? When I said that I am from small town, at that time you said that I was a good guy; but when things are rough, you are saying this." I said weeping.

"Yeah! I was wrong. Everyone told me not to befriend such a boy. I never listened to anyone. Now I am. . ."

I interrupted, "Why are you saying this? I said sorry many times. I am sorry for what I did. Please forgive me and please come back to me," I pleaded.

"Come back? You are insane. You say you love me, but if you did then you would have never said those things. Huh, love me. A guy like you could slap me. And what do you have? You have nothing. You are a poor chap. At least Ram Sharma had a big house and is a single child of his parents. You have nothing. And I know you can do nothing. I made a mistake. I should have accepted his proposal." Her voice was rising and becoming shriller, unbearable and heart wrenching after each word.

"How could you forget all those things, those lovely things and those talks? And I will crack IIT. Please stay with me. Please don't say all this. It hurts," I said.

"It also hurts me when you were throwing your poison that day. All were lies and illusions. Go and first crack IIT and then I will come. And don't try to contact Tulika and my friends, otherwise it'll be bad for you. It is better that I change my batch in tuition. I don't want to see you."

"Illusion? Lie? How could you say this? How heartless you have become! Why would you change? I will change. Already you have made a lot of mistakes. I will shift my batch. You don't need to do this." This time my patience wore a little. It was unbearable to hear her words.

I was listening patiently to her and it became too much, then I said, "You said to the others that I am just time pass for you. You talked to everyone in school and said something else to me. Someone told me that you chat with a boy; he proposed you and you still continued talking to him. You lied so glibly that I couldn't smell it. You broke my trust in this relationship."

She remained silent for a moment, then said, "Why are you worrying so much? We spent only a year and we are also not physical? Then, why are you worrying so much."

"Physical! I have never dreamt such a thing in life." I was startled. My nerves, it seemed, have got paralyzed. She left nothing more for me to say.

I realized the acerbity of her words, stabbing me so hard that I burst into tears. "I love you, I love you very much," I managed to say. It was terrible. Voices started echoing in my ears: "You have nothing. All were lies." And I wailed and broke down into tears – endless tears.

Before I could say something, a hissing sound made me realize that she slammed down the phone and it went dead with a "*Fuck off!*"

I was astounded as her words trembled in my heart, my senses; it seemed a knife had been stabbed into my heart. I slipped myself on a chair, beside the table, with my mouth agape.

◆

Next day in class, for the first two hours, everyone was in the computer lab, but my mind was wandering over her words. How many times, I forced myself to believe that it was a bad dream.

The words were still piercing. I buried myself into books, but was lost somewhere.

"Hello," she said. It was Ritika.

"Oh! Hello," I said barely audible.

"Hello, what happened? Are you okay? You look dull. Did Ashima call you? Did she say anything to you?" she said. Her voice rose shrilly in concern. "Are you okay?"

"Sort of," I said. My throat was chocked. I was sobbing.

"Aarush, are you okay? I know she called you. Tell me."

"Yeah! She called and scolded me. She said that I am a narrow minded one and abused me endlessly and asked me to crack IIT, and then she would come and explain everything."

"Hush! Hush... Aarush, please! You don't look good when you cry. Please smile," she said, trying to reassure me. "From now onwards, you are not going to talk to her." After a moment of silence, she added, "You really are not going to talk to her."

"But how will I live without her? Without talking to her?" I said in a broken tone, and few words dissolved in the sob. "She was saying that she will change the batch. I stopped her. I am going to change my batch. I don't want to be a problem for her. You know I go to hostel through DPS, so that I can just see her."

"I know you love her much. I know, but changing the batch, you would do whatever she will say. I know how possessive you are about her. She sometimes told me about you. I was pleased to hear this that she got so lucky to be with you, but now..."

"Whatever she had said... she doesn't love me now. Those bitter words are enough to pierce, to shatter my hope, to wreck my dreams, my heart, my feelings. She even declared them to be illusions and lies, but I must tell you she loved me – not now – not for the whole time, but she loved me. I know the mehendi and those conversations were not easy for any girl," I said, in a droopy tone. "You know, whatever she said, I don't mind. I just wish she'd come back to my life. If she says sorry once, even if she doesn't feel sorry, I wouldn't mind. I just want her to come back."

"She will."

I kept calm for a long time, but later, I couldn't control myself hiding those feelings from others, even from Ritika. Finally, I broke down. "You know, I always wondered what was love? What happens when one is in love? You know love had never come to me so easily. I watched it in movies and inferred. Love is a beautiful thing, an adorable feeling. It makes your life complete; it shapes your life and gives you an inspiration to live. It is unbiased. Love unites two souls together, and fills it with excessive zeal and happiness, cares to last a lifetime till both of them live together. Love brings happiness in life; it removes the grief of each time, and soothes your feelings and emotions. A feeling which can't be measured; it only can be felt, which I felt when she came into my life like an angel to fill the void, which I always felt throughout my life. When she walked into my life, I was so happy that I couldn't measure my happiness. Throughout the days we were together, it looked like Ashima was the girl I was looking for. I was happy that I could share my emotions and feelings with her. I discovered the aspect of life, the hidden beauty in the form of Ashima who loved me. My excitement and happiness were out of control. It seemed right that good things come to those who wait. For me, it was the best thing I get which I always wished to keep and love forever, but it faded away. But after knowing all those things about her, it has proven that what I thought about love was all wrong. You know, not a single tinge of hate crawled in my heart for her. Love is the best thing until things get wrong, it hurts, tortures and makes you to cry a lot, then nothing can be worse than this. It is painful. Who knows this better than me? It looks that worlds starts falling upon you; you dreams, emotions, your feelings, everything breaks and become worthless for others. But love is a small fight also followed by forgiveness and lives the same life again. I am not saying that I didn't do anything. I also made mistakes. I apologize for my slip of tongue on that day. I never wished to say any of those hurtful things to her. But you also know how does it feel when one sees his or her lover with someone else? She never gave me a chance to apologize. Even she didn't care for my feelings, my emotions, even after knowing that I would shatter emotionally without her. I just want to live with her. I never believe in time pass. I always wished that whom I'd love, I will marry too. I wish to live together like before... cheerfully and happily. As you probably know, I kept the fidelity of the relationship. The relations which require effort to be maintained are never true, and if relations are true, they never require any effort to be maintained. I started feeling that love is a damaging mistake and its accomplices – hope, faith, trust – a treacherous illusion," I bewailed, staring somewhere very distant, lost somewhere. My eyes were blurry with tears and one thick drop streaked down which I had tried to hold for a long time.

Ritika wiped my tears.

My eyes rolled with a glint of gratefulness over her face. Her eyes were also moist and face was calm. "Thanks."

"So sweet of you. How much do you think about her? Why do you blame yourself for what happened? She hasn't been her usual perky self? Her persona is quite different from what she is. For some people, how is it possible to maintain the façade of love or lust? And on other hand, for someone it is possible to be a sculpture of love, care and affection. You know some people don't understand this. They think love is a game to play with someone's emotions. When they wish, they will come and go. I accept love is not always hunky dory. But people have to understand that life is not always the same. There are ups and downs. But through all of this, one thing should not change – the feeling of love," she said. "Your love is so true, a true and pure feeling. I am sure she will come to you. What more should I say? Your words made me speechless and made me think that really, does there really exists a boy who loves his girlfriend so much?" She gave an encouraging pat on my back and put her assuring arm around my shoulder. I felt a little embarrassed and put it aside.

"You are too good to me."

"I know. I am too good to you because you are too good for anyone. I hope we had met earlier," she said and giggled. She often said these types of sentences, so that I could giggle and come out of my somber mood. "Don't worry whether she will come back to you or not. I will propose to you and you have to accept my proposal."

First I was embarrassed, and then I giggled.

"Promise me that you will not talk to her. And if she tries to hurt you, I will surely slap her hard." Her last sentence came with a little seriousness and I peered at her and saw that her face had unnaturally twisted, unlike before.

Despite her encouragement, I was daunted by the awareness that my pain would not ebb away easily.

The series of tears trailed on my cheeks. I went to wash my face. I checked myself in the mirror. My eyes were sullen and pale. My lips were dry. I washed my face and came into the classroom.

When I thought about her, my eyes pricked with tears. I felt nostalgic and lost control over myself. The pain was too much to bear.

I changed my tuition batch. I even changed my way to school. Another day, I saw her sister in market; it made me hopeful that she would also be around, but I couldn't find her. I went to the same place again and again in hope that she would also come with her and I would catch a glimpse of her, but she never came. Images of couples on the roadside, their giggling while walking to tuition started dancing unendingly before my eyes and started reminding me of her. Her image in every girl made me very anxious and raised my pain; subsequently I even stopped going to the market.

◆

The news of my break-up soon spread up from DPS to Chinmaya. To my surprise, a wide variety of rumours reached my ears. I ignored every such rumour except one that I had berated and abused Ashima, though she talked to me very diligently and I dumped her even after this.

Every morning, I woke up long before dawn and lay exhausted and wakeful, with eyes closed, thinking of the countless years I still had to live without her. There were no more missed calls, no long conversations, no more 'I love yous' and giggles and no fights about who would disconnect the phone first. No more jokes to giggleat. All that was left was a bundle of memories and her smiling face. There was hardly any moment when I wasn't thinking of her; actually there was not a single moment. My pain was becoming deeper and harsher which I never felt before. It climbed to my head from my heart and soon, it became pervasive and intense, which I was unable to endure. It was no less debilitating, leaving me barely able to stand on my feet. It led me finally to my bed, forcing me to lie like a corpse. Day after day, the pain became fatal, eating me up.

Every second, a wave of affection overcame me. My heart filled with reminiscence, and I was pondering about her, her pinkish cheeks, dimpled smiling cheeks, hair ruffled by air, and eyes filled with enormous love.

I could smell her, sense her presence. My mind was always with her, looking for her, distant. I sensed her smell. Did I? I didn't know whom I was talking to. I saw myself desolate and alone.

I groaned at the memory, suffering all over again. "Go away. Go away. Let me live," I squeaked. With deliberate and desperate effort, I sent the tendril of thoughts out of my mind and body. I struggled with those thoughts. Lovely thoughts were bullying me, leading to an aching emptiness in my heart. I could no longer distinguish between reality and illusion, between love and attraction.

With her memories, my headache was increasing day by day.

In between, I bunked the mid-terms and went to Siwan for a medical check-up.

◆

"Where have you been? I tried your cell phone so many times. It was switched off or you didn't respond. I ask where you have been?" Ritika complained breathlessly.

"Calm down, Ritika. I went for a check-up," I said slowly.

She looked calm now and said quietly, "At least, you could have informed me. Why would you inform me? I know I am not your friend. Who am I for you?"

"It is not like that. I went suddenly. And I stayed at my friend's home, so I couldn't call you. I am sorry. Will you not ask me how I am?" I said.

"What did the doctor say? Are you all right now?" she asked in her usual tone, sweet and soothing. Her tone was showing her eagerness.

"He advised me to rest. Even asked me to keep away from the studies for a while. Doctors don't know anything," I smiled.

"Oh yeah, they don't know anything. You know everything. Listen, just follow his advice. And have the medicine as per his direction, otherwise I am going to scold you," she said and smiled.

"Indeed. Whatever you say. Now smile," I requested.

In between, my birthday came. Firoz wished me first. Ritika called me at 12:01 a.m. She was annoyed that she couldn't wish me first.

I waited the whole day and night, but Ashima didn't call me; she did not even message me. I faded into melancholy.

I even sent her some chocolates through Ritika.

◆

The same evening, Ritika went to Ashima's home.

"Hello, aunty. Is Ashima there?" said Ritika soon after opening the door.

"Oh, Ritika, it has been a long time since you came here. How is your mummy and papa?" Ashima's mother said.

"Everything is fine at home," Ritika said with a smile and moved towards Ashima's room.

"Hey, Ashima. What are you doing?" Ritika said.

"Nothing much. After a long time," Ashima said without any expression on her face.

"Hmm. But what decision did you make? What do you think?" Ritika asked, sitting on a chair near her bed.

"What decision?" Ashima seemed indigenous. "Oh, now I see what you mean? No, I won't talk to him. That's why you are here?" Her voice turned salty.

"Why are you doing this to him? I know everything. He made mistakes; that cannot be reversed. It is not about fun; it is about something deeper," said Ritika.

"So you think of me as guilty. Instead of pulling a long face and glaring at me, why don't you accept that what he said was not right," said Ashima. It became a topic of debate instead of discussion.

"But he loves you more than his life. He is so lovely; he is very special for you," said Ritika.

"Huh! If he loves me, than how could he ask me to strip before my friends and talk? At that time, he didn't care for my feelings, then why I should I care for him?"

"You don't care, but he cares for you. It was just a slip of tongue. For that you can't torture such a pure and divine heart. You don't see him. He hasn't said much to me, but I have seen him, crying for you the whole day in class. He always looks so lost in your memories. Ashima, you are so lucky that someone cries for you, someone care for you so much. How could you forget those lovely days you both have spent?" said Ritika, choosing her words well.

"Then, how did he forget his love at the time of shouting at me?" argued Ashima.

"He has not forgotten anything. He feels sorry all the time. And he endures the pain stoically without letting you know. Ashima, you will never know the meaning of love. You always flirted with other boys. You know, after knowing everything about your sleazy acts, he didn't say anything and doesn't have even a tinge of hatred for you. He said that his only wish is to live with you, to share the same moments and the same joy. You will never know the meaning of love. You are so unlucky."

Ashima didn't say anything. A long silence followed before Ashima said, "Huh! How would you understand what I felt when he said it at that time? It hurts me even now. He made a mistake and he has to pay for it."

"Right, and you are hurting him more than he deserves, because he loves you more than you deserve and about mistakes, you are quite right that he made mistakes. He made the mistake of loving you, caring for you, of keeping you at the top of his desire. He made mistakes by making a dream, a castle where he sees only you, where you are a princess and he is a prince, but he doesn't know that the castle he is making is of sand, and soon that is going to be swept away," said Ritika and her voice became so emotional that tears rolled down her eyes.

"He is so lovely, and sweet that anyone can love him far more than you did. I have seen love for you in his eyes, and I know no one can take your place in his life. Please come back to Aarush. By the way, he has sent chocolates for you on his birthday, but you don't have respect for anything so I will take them back," saying that, Ritika closed the door softly behind her.

Next day in class, Ritika didn't say anything about this, nor about the chocolates, but her face simply said everything that brought despair to me and I didn't ask anything at all.

20

My studies were completely out of track and I had missed lots of topics in the syllabus. I started going to school regularly and tuition too. I joined the brilliant test series for IIT JEE. Ritika supported me every time, whether it was a class or in the tuition. She helped me to copy down notes. I accustomed myself to this tentative and pleasant friendship. Sometimes, she teased me badly.

One day, the class was free. Everyone was having lunch. She came to me. I was lost somewhere thinking of something, maybe in memories of Ashima.

"Aarush! Aarush!" Ritika shouted near my ears after calling me several times. I jumped suddenly.

"Oh, it's you? Hello, done with your lunch?" I asked.

"No, what are you doing here sitting alone? I know you are missing her," she said but continued to talk. "I have something for you. If you are happy, then I'll give a very important thing to you."

"What?"

"Ah! It's a secret. First smile like a good boy, then you get the present that I bought for you."

"See, I am smiling a broad smile. Now, give me that present." I tried to smile as much as I could.

"Not now, tomorrow. I haven't brought it today."

I waited impatiently for the next day. The whole night, I tried to figure it out, but I wasn't successful. Next day, when I reached school, Ritika was already waiting for me. I just jumped up, reached her and asked, "Now, the wait is over. Give me. See, I am still smiling. See my white teeth."

"Ok, come."

I followed her like a good boy who followed his parents in hope to get sweets. She turned to me with a wrapped gift in her hand.

"What is this?" I said before my heart pound.

"The diary, which Ashima gave to you long ago," she said. "I know she took it back from you by tricking you."

"Where did you get this?" I was surprised. It was almost unbelievable.

"Actually, when I went to her home to convince her, I saw this diary on her desk. First, I was in no mood to take it, but when she was in no mood to listen to my words, I had to take it," she said in a childish tone. "Literally, I stole it for you."

"Yes, you did very well. You don't know what you have brought for me. You have put life back in a corpse. You are so wise, so wonderful, and so lovely." My happiness flooded out.

With a smile, she handed the diary to me.

I anxiously opened the diary. Nothing new was there. I diligently turned each page three times in a hope to get something, get some words from her, but I couldn't find anything. She had torn out each photo of hers from the pages, and that saddened me. Seeing this diary I wanted to meet her once. Maybe from a distance, I just wished one look of her.

There was silence. During this silent interlude, I remarked that the pain of not seeing Ashima had been far more than I would suffer on seeing her.

I wrapped the diary in the same paper and kept it in the bag. I turned towards Ritika. She was observing me, but soon, her loving

gaze faded looking at my face which was no longer radiant. She understood my pain, but didn't say anything. I tried to smile, but couldn't do it so sincerely and it was a mere upturning of my lips.

Coming back to the hostel, I read the diary again and again. It seemed as if a lost desert traveller had just found an oasis. I fell asleep reading and remembering the incidents written in the diary.

In the coming days, there were moments when the clouds of my pain disperse into laughter with the other school students in the class.

One day in the class when the other students were busy eating their lunch, Tanmay was cracking cheap jokes and laughing at Rashmi. I was on the last desk and turning the pages of a novel. Ritika came to me and handed me her lunch box.

"Aarush, lunch for you," she said.

"No, I am full. And please don't do so much for me. I won't be able to repay you," I said closing the book.

"I also didn't want to bring lunch for you, but when my mother packed it, it smelled so good that I couldn't resist. If you don't want to eat, then don't eat." She averted her eyes and said in a tone of anger garnished with softness, not intended to hurt me. "I know you haven't had any breakfast in the morning."

I was surprised about how she came to know that I hadn't had breakfast. She said that she knew everything about me. When I asked questions, she answered all of them.

"Arre yaar, you know too much about me. Ok, tell me my favourite idea for a date. It's a tough one. I know you wouldn't be able to answer," I smiled mockingly.

"You and Ashima in a candle light dinner on Saturday night in a five-star restaurant with soft romantic music playing in the background. You would be in a black suit and Ashima in a red

gown. And after dinner, you both will have a ball dance." She said in one tone. Her words grew with a very unusual passion.

I felt shy hearing this. I was agape. *How does she know this*?

"You won. You know a lot about me." I smiled, opening the lunch box.

It was soyabean chilli and roti. I felt shy eating in front of her so I turned back.

"Aarush, can I ask you something?"

"Yeah, sure," I noticed something peculiar, not the same friendly gaze; her voice was also different.

"Do you still find her pretty? Do you still love her?"

At first, I was amazed to listen to this. This question was quite irrelevant at that time, but I remained silent. I know, the answer was 'yes'.

"Why?" I asked.

"Answer me."

I was forced by her to answer. Looking at her, at her serious tone and cold gaze, I said calmly, "I don't know."

"Don't know! Okay, I will ask something more. Did you both ever do anything out of order?"

"Out of order?"

She smiled little, but I felt the seriousness in her tone and coldness in her gaze.

"What are you talking about?"

I gave her a puzzled look as though I didn't understand.

"Kiss… or… something like that!" she whispered.

"What? Are you mad? What happened to you today? Are you okay?" I never expected such questions from her.

"Tell me. You can't conceal anything from your good friend and I hope I am your good friend."

"You are a very good friend of mine," I said. "No, never... it happened. In fact, you know about us more than I do."

"Did you put your hand somewhere it doesn't belong?"

"What?" This time, I was agape. "Have you become mad? I am going." And I left that place.

What happened to Ritika? I was completely astonished by her questions. I will never discuss these things with her.

But I found a difference in her thereafter – she started caring for me, in fact, she started bringing lunch for me. I always thought of her as a good friend (might be the best friend).

Ashima's presence apparently started fading away. But I was still impatient to hear about her. But I never asked Ritika about this.

She never left me alone, not in the classroom at least. But this effort couldn't fill the vaccum created by Ashima's absence from my life, though I never talked to her about Ashima.

Whenever I was about to hang up the phone, Ritika always said bye with same gracious tone, and "We could talk a little more but, no problem. Come to school tomorrow. We will have a good time. I call you when my parents aren't home. Bye. Take care!"

The anguish of love disciplined me and brought some maturity within me. It felt good among friends, but it never made me to forget Ashima and my pain.

◆

Days slipped into weeks, and weeks into months. Ashima's birthday was coming. Also this time, I wanted to wish her the first, how could I?

"She must have a mobile. Should I call her? But I want to wish her first. I know she doesn't love me, but I love her," I thought and brooded over this thought, a day before Ashima's birthday.

"One thing I can do... I can message her," I thought and smiled at my own plan to wish her first.

I wrote a message with a sweet birthday cake MMS which I had downloaded the previous night. I didn't write my name so that I didn't become a problem later. I waited for 11:59:45 p.m. I sent the message. Luckily, it got delivered at 11:59:59 p.m.

No phone. No reply. Nothing. I also didn't do anything. I didn't want to upset her, not on her birthday.

In between, I appeared for the NDA exam.

I got a call letter for an interview. It was in the month of January that I went to Bangalore. I quit the interview on the third day and came back. I had no reason for this and I didn't explain this to anyone.

The board exam's date had been announced. It was about to start from the 1st of March.

I forced myself to study, but didn't do too well in maths.

On the last day of examination, all our classmates met for the last time. Everyone was greeting each other. Hugs. Photographs. Slam books. Those were very emotional moments for us. We had seen so many wonderful moments together in Chinmaya. Now the time had come for separation. Every eye was moist. Mine too. Everyone was making promises to meet at least once in a year to form the same realm of love and togetherness we had shown throughout our time in school.

I too shook hands with the other girls. Finally, I came to meet my best friend, Ritika Dey. She stood a little distant from the others in a corner. Her eyes were moist. No longer a luminous face. No more the jovial smile. No glint in those innocent big eyes.

"How was your exam?" I asked.

"It was okay. Yours?" she said, keeping her tone low and without any emotion.

"Not so good. English! You know," I said in a jocular way but she didn't laugh, didn't even smile.

"So your handshakes and photographs are over?" she asked, narrowing her eyes.

"Not yet. Still left," I tried again, at least to make her smile. As I had never seen her this way, I forwarded my slam book.

She signed and put a smiley and returned it to me.

"So you are going?" she said ruefully. "Is this the last time we are meeting?"

"I am not going back right away. After IIT and AIEEE. But I promise that I will come every year to meet you, to meet my best friend."

"But you are going anyhow." Her voice grew gloomy.

"I will miss your smile. Your innocent laugh. Your hair style. Your friendship. Your talks. And in one word – you."

"Haan, I will miss you. Very much." I smiled.

She also smiled, with tearful eyes. I wiped her tears. "Now, smile."

She nodded and said, "Promise me that you will call me every day." I smiled. "Always put that smile on your face, you look good when you smile and like adevil when you are sad."

"Ritika, I want to say something to you."

"Hmm. Say."

"It is unforgettable for me, the time spent with you is one of the most precious times for me. I don't know how I should thank you. Whatever you have done for me is immeasurable. You don't know but you have made me laugh; you taught me how to live a life full of courage, energy which I lost somewhere. You did everything for me."

"Now, let's go. The others are waiting for a group photo." And we moved.

At last, we all took a group photo. And promised to be in contact with each other.

I also turned back for the hostel. Just before leaving, I turned back to look at Ritika. She was still there and I smiled.

On the way back, I saw Mayank and Smriti laughing together, though she was unaware that he was cheating on her.

How ironical.

In the coming days, the other competitive exams got over. For the last time with little hope, I called Aachanakya on the landline, but hearing her mother's voice destroyed my last wish to hear her. I desperately wanted to meet her. It had been ten months since I had seen or spoken to her.

Epilogue

The bus stops with a sudden shudder, almost jolting me out.

I look outside. The same shops, same roads, films posters are glued to the public wall. Nothing new has happened in these two years. I have reached Siwan.

"Wake up everyone," Firoz shouts, dragging his luggage out. "Pick up your bags!"

My tears have dried. Eyes are sullen. Carrying my luggage in my hand, I come out of the bus. I see my father who is waiting for me. He has come to receive me. After bidding goodbye to everyone, I go to my home.

The days are passing. She has never called me in these months and I cannot dare to call her again. Earlier, I couldn't feel the love, but at least it was not that painful. But now, life is not the same anymore. Whenever I think about this, it upsets me. How true, in course of true love... I am left with nothing!

Recommended Reading

Her Last Wish

Ajay K Pandey

His father's over expectations only ruined his self-confidence further with each failure. A ray of hope walked into his life as his wife. Everything is going per plan, when he finds out that she does not have much time to live and takes it upon himself to fight all odds – even his family, if need be – to help her fight her medical condition.

Her Last Wish is an inspiring story of love, relationships and sacrifice.

Ajay is the bestselling author of *You are the Best Wife* and has won many hearts with his writing. He is also actively involved in working for social causes.

ISBN: 978-9382665878; Price: 175/-; Pages: 208; Binding: Paperback.

You are my Reason to Smile

Arpit Vageria

Ranbir is a dreamer. He has a well-paying job, is a good lover, an ideal son, but he is not happy. Because his true calling is not in the corporate; it's in writing. Amidst all this confusion, Pihu Sharma enters his life – his first ever fan, who seems to be head over heels in love with him. Join Ranbir as he makes his way through a world that kills for money and dies for love.

Arpit Vageria is a bestselling author of *I Still Think About You*. He also writes for the Indian television industry, and enjoys road trips, singing, playing pranks and adventurous sports.

ISBN: 978-9382665885; Price: 175/-; Pages: 184; Binding: Paperback.

Promise Me A Million Times

Keshav Aneel

Like a couple of migratory birds, both Charlie and Edwin leave to settle in the big city. For Edwin, it was to chase his dreams of becoming an actor; but for Charlie, it was just to be with his only friend.

Life throws Charlie in Aster's way. He could never have guessed, but he was in for an absolute unthoughtful phase of profoundness, which was going to last forever.

Keshav Aneel is a young marketing professional, who chose to do his heart's bidding and ended his brief corporate career to immerse himself into his creative side.

ISBN: 978-93-82665-73-1; Price: 175/-; Pages: 168; Binding: Paperback.

No Matter What I Do

Devanshi Sharma

Kabir, Amaira, Kushank and Suhani – four very different people bound together by love and friendship – are struggling to find the motto of their lives. Four threads entangled together and four lives recuperating each other – *No Matter What I Do* is the story of these four youngsters, on a journey to find themselvesand how they reverse stereotypes on the way.

Devanshi Sharma is a twenty-one-year-old dreamer from Indore and strongly believes in hope. She enjoys talking, writing, dancing and eating, and her family is her lifeline.

ISBN: 978-9382665847; Price: 175/-; Pages: 200; Binding: Paperback.

Twenty Twenty: A Race Against Time

Anuraag Srivastava

Abhi and Aditi are siblings who want to realise their dreams in the big city. In the midst of all the struggle and success, if they are not able to resolve a crisis in twenty days, their very existence can come under threat. In short, they have to hit sixes on every bouncer thrown at them.

Twenty Twenty is a story of betrayal, deceit and relationships, where a master planner devises games, to get to his own ambitions.

Anuraag Srivastava has been a banker for over eighteen years now. Presently based at Ghaziabad, he is a poet, guitarist, photographer and avid reader.

ISBN: 9789382665915; Pages: 224; MRP: INR 195/-; Binding: Paperback

---

Messed Up! But All For Love

Arvind Parashar

Neil and Gauri are deeply in love, but Neil's fitness consultant Srinya seems to be stirring some trouble in their lives. Drishti is a TV news anchor and journalist and her husband Somesh, a top cop. They bump into Neil and his friends in Cuba and things change.

The havoc ensues when Drishti gets abducted and Neil is framed for it.

In short, their lives are *Messed Up! But All for Love*.

Arvind Parashar is has been a corporate leader in firms like GE, Dell and Genpact. He is a painter who enjoys road trips and gives motivational lectures.

ISBN: 9789382665946; Pages: 176; MRP: INR 175/-; Binding: Paperback